CREATED EQUAL

I hope you enjoy the story!

Roger

Created Equal

A Novel

By Roger A. Brown

Curran Press
Rockport, Massachusetts

ISBN 978-1-970002-08-9 (hardcover) and 978-1-970002-09-6 (paperback)
www.rogerabrown.com

Dedicated to my family
headed by Linda
without whose support I am unable to do anything.

CHAPTER ONE

Allie's heart was beating so loudly it finally woke her up. It felt like an eternity, this effort to regain consciousness. Her temples stung, her mouth felt hot and metallic, and her heart throbbed like it was lodged inside her head.

A faint impression intruded in her brain—she was supposed to be somewhere else. People were waiting for her. Someone was depending on her. But who? The impression disappeared in the time it took to exhale a single breath. She tried to ignore the stimuli intruding on her senses; surely she must be at home. Where else would she be?

Slowly her mind started to swim towards the surface of awareness. She felt her face resting on something. She moved her head, seeking the serene asylum of the pillow. Whatever it was, it was rough to her skin. Allie always slept on her side, this she knew. Finally, at that moment, she had a sense of herself.

She was sitting upright. She tried to move her arms and legs, but was unable. She looked down and saw that her head had been resting forward on a piece of unfinished lumber;

under it her arms and legs lie straight out in wooden stocks. She tried to pull her arms free, but the openings were not big enough. Her legs were lying on a wide bench attached at right angles to the leg stocks. She leaned backward, but felt nothing behind her.

A void. Whoever did this made sure she would remain in an upright sitting position indefinitely. She was in good physical shape, but she realized her lower back was starting to ache. Where was she?

She was not outside. The flickering lights, which in an already-distant memory seemed like stars in the sky, were too large, huddled too close together . . . candles. Allie was no stranger to candles. She knew these candles, but so many? Someone had lit them. It would take a while.

She began to feel fear. Not the fear of something she could recognize, like a spider or a snake. Those fears could be rationalized. This was a different fear, something unknown. Fear was exciting—fear galvanized into action. This was resignation. Dread. She knew instinctively that whomever lit all these candles had plans for her, eliciting fears in her that could not be rationalized. Dread transformed into the slow burn of terror.

"Get a grip," she said to herself. Aloud? Allie wasn't sure. Beyond terror there was only one more level: panic. *Don't give in.*

"Agnus dei . . . agnus dei . . . agnus dei." The sound of her heart pounding in her ears was replaced by an eerie chanting sound. "Agnus dei . . . agnus dei . . . agnus dei." The Latin from middle school entered her mind like it was yesterday. "Lamb of God."

As she peered intently into the darkness for a clue, a dark shape came into focus. The flickering glow of light around it seemed to reflect off a shiny surface. Her mind began to search for answers. There was just enough light that she could barely see a reflection. She squinted, trying to identify what seemed to be a large black cross reflecting off the floor.

Her mind was playing tricks. It wasn't a cross at all. It was a silhouette, a dark silhouette lying prostrate on the floor with outspread arms. As the eerie chant pounded louder in her ears, a large man rose in front of her. He was dressed in priestly robes, emaciated, with a full black beard, a shaven head, and coal-black eyes that reflected the light of a hundred candles. Panic began to seep into her bones like winter's first chill.

Allie knew he could see her. She just hoped he couldn't hear the relentless pounding of her heart.

So many miles. She had done this before. The need to focus. All those miles, all those hills. She focused only on the sound of her own breath. She was so afraid. She needed to transform the panic into pain. Pain she could deal with; pain was easy.

She bit sharply into her lip. The more the pain increased, the more her breathing relaxed and the more calm she would feel. Mile 20, hitting the wall. Two quick breaths, in through the nose. One long exhale, out through the mouth. Repeat. The harder she bit, the calmer she felt. More pain, less panic. Slowly, staring up the hill. Feeling the joy of a single step. Relaxing into it. Climbing that mountain.

No more throbbing in the ears. He couldn't hear her anymore. Slowly, she felt her heart rate start to subside.

As Allie listened to the evil droning on, her vision finally became more clear. She didn't know who this madman was, but she knew what he wanted. He wanted to stop her and there was only one way to do that. *It didn't matter anymore,* she thought. Whether she survived or not, she knew she had already won.

With synapses exploding, endorphins rushing, and lips slowly moistening with blood, she allowed herself the briefest, most imperceptible hint of a smile.

CHAPTER TWO

FIVE WEEKS EARLIER . . .

As Tommy Riley finished his last sip of coffee, he neatly folded *The Times-Picayune* and tossed it in the recycling bin. He rinsed out his cup, sprayed his plate spotless with near-boiling water, and put them both in the dishwasher. Washing the dishes to put them in the dishwasher, his father used to joke. Tommy was still his mother's son through and through; her lessons on tidiness were inescapable.

As he stared at his reflection in the bathroom mirror, he noticed that his face had very few wrinkles. Although he wouldn't call himself vain, he worked hard to stay fit. It was more about how he felt. The extra layer of belly that wouldn't go away—a gift, no doubt, from his Italian grandfather—he hid well with an easy style and well-tailored suits. It was, after all, New Orleans; skinny men were not to be trusted. Nevertheless, the years of rowing on Bayou St. John had paid off. At six feet three inches and a solid 195 pounds, he was pleasantly lean, with broad shoulders and the muscle tone of a much younger man.

He brushed his teeth and combed his hair. Tommy was more than happy to let whomever he was dating at the time take charge of his hair, as long as it was appropriate for court. He liked this look Nikki had come up with, gleaned most likely from some movie star of which he was unaware. Of course, the darkish hair of his youth was turning to salt and pepper. Women seemed to love it, though he wasn't sure why. In fact, women loved Tommy Riley since the first day he could remember. Always had and he guessed probably always would.

Opening the heavy, wooden closet door in his bedroom, he scanned his large wardrobe and picked out an impeccably-tailored, light-gray Paul Smith suit from Rubensteins. He paired it with a pink Zegna shirt and a light-blue silk tie with pink flowers that bespoke of its designer, Hermès. Finally, he pulled on a pair of hand-made black ostrich boots; a souvenir, he thought fondly, of his time in Texas. A refined taste in attire was one of the many things he'd picked up from Joe Bob.

After graduating from law school in Austin, Tommy had gone to work for Joe Bob Finley as an associate. Joe Bob was one of the top plaintiff's lawyers in Texas and only took cases when the defendants had deep pockets. Product liability, personal injury, high-profile divorces; he took them all . . . and sometimes the divorcées, too. It was a small law firm with no partners, just Joe Bob and a small staff of associate lawyers to do the grunt work. There was always endless legal research, motion dockets, preparation of pleadings, and anything else that Joe Bob deemed necessary. Almost immediately, Tommy displayed the promise Joe Bob had seen in him. He soon began trying his own lawsuits with great success—and attracting his own clients.

Ten years after Tommy's graduation from law school, he became Joe Bob's first and only law partner. When the Code of Ethics had been liberalized to allow attorneys to advertise, Tommy took full advantage. The fact that he had been a notable football player at UT had helped him immensely. Tommy Riley was on a roll. Joe Bob and Tommy agreed to split everything the firm brought in fifty-fifty.

Joe Bob and Tommy were similar in many ways. Of course, they argued about everything. Joe Bob was an A&M man, a fact that rankled Tommy, but only served to broaden their appeal.

The biggest difference was in their relationships with women. Neither had a problem finding attractive, available women who were more than willing to date. It was Texas and it was the 1990s. But the length of their relationships differed greatly. Tommy always found a way to extricate himself from the lady of the moment whenever talk ventured into the tricky territory of long-term commitment. Joe Bob, on the other hand, was a big fan of marriage. He did it often. He even carried a three-carat engagement ring in the pocket of his suit coat at all times; he never knew when it might come in handy for a sudden proposal.

When a beautiful woman of moderate intelligence, quick wit, and vivacious attitude told Joe Bob that her only goal in life was to make him happy forever, his ego gave him no choice but to believe her. That same ego would also not allow him to even consider a prenuptial agreement.

Practice in this case did not make perfect. Only after the fourth Mrs. Finley had left for greener pastures—taking a significant amount of Joe Bob's greener property with her—did Joe Bob lose all sense of romance. Accordingly, Joe Bob became a favorite client of the most elite female escort services of Houston—and Dallas, Atlanta, and Miami as well. Surprisingly, he found those relationships were as meaningful as any of those he had with the four Mrs. Finleys, were considerably less complicated, and a whole lot cheaper.

Successful law careers from the beginning, it was in the late 1990s that Joe Bob and Tommy's fortunes changed significantly. The heart that Joe Bob had poured out to so many juries, the heart that he had given so carelessly to all the women he loved and thought he loved—that heart suddenly gave out. When Tommy heard the news that Joe Bob had died *in flagrante* with his boots off, he was duly saddened. But he was also happy knowing that Joe Bob died doing one of the two things he loved most.

At the time of Joe Bob's untimely demise, tobacco litigation had been a focal point across the country in every state attorney general's office. Armed with the deadly effects of tobacco and the additional cost of related diseases burdening Medicaid, states began to seek recourse from tobacco companies. The attorney general of Texas began the process of interviewing trial lawyers for the plaintiff in search of the best in the state to pursue action against big tobacco. Five attorneys were selected to file the action in Texarkana, Texas, a well-known jurisdiction for rendering higher than normal monetary judgments on behalf of plaintiffs.

Under the arrangement, the lawyers were to bear all expenses and would receive a contingency fee based upon their success. Failure meant millions of dollars and years of irreplaceable time down the drain, but the potential reward outweighed the risk. After three years of litigation and the plaintiff's lawyers having spent over thirty million dollars of their own money, the state of Texas received an award in excess of 17 billion dollars. The five lawyers were each awarded additional fees from the tobacco companies of 3.3 billion dollars. Three other states received judgments against the tobacco companies; unlike in Texas, however, attorneys in those states received millions instead of billions. Shortly after the Texas decision, forty-six other states settled with the tobacco companies in an amount exceeding 200-billion dollars overall; at the time, it was the largest transfer of wealth in the nation's history.

Joe Bob and Tommy's firm had not been named in the elite group that became known as the Tobacco Five. But one of Joe Bob's old law-school classmates was. And when faced with the substantial costs of continuing a lawsuit with such questionable results, he decided to bring in another firm to share the burden. He approached Joe Bob and Tommy. Since the tobacco companies had only lost two cases that had been filed for related diseases in the United States, the odds were long. Joe Bob was used to long odds because that was what a plaintiff's trial lawyer's life was all about. A loss meant nothing; but a win, well, that's why God made contingency fees. They went for half and hit the jackpot. Unfortunately, Joe Bob wouldn't live to enjoy it. But Tommy ended up with more money than he could ever spend in a lifetime.

CHAPTER THREE

After dressing, Tommy called down to the lobby. "Good morning, George. Will you please have my car brought to the front?"

Tommy knew the phrase "ethical lawyer" was an oxymoron to some, but it wasn't for lack of trying on his part. He had purchased his first Lincoln Navigator the year the government bailed out General Motors and Chrysler. Since Lincoln, owned by Ford, didn't need any taxpayers' dollars, he decided to reward them by trading in his German made luxury car the day after the bailout. He tried to spend his considerable wealth ethically.

It was this same reasoning that led him to form the Riley Law Group. After the tobacco payout, money was no longer a concern. He entrusted his fortune to Peter James, a high-school football teammate and longtime friend with an MBA in finance from Wharton. He had sharp instincts in the investment markets. Peter stimulated the growth of Tommy's investment income until it greatly exceeded his personal needs.

Tommy loved little things such as good wine and whiskey, high-quality sushi and steak, and a fine suit. He also enjoyed a fast car and the occasional trip to Paris. But when it came to mansions and airplanes, yachts and jewelry, Tommy had little inclination. In short, Tommy found he had more money than he could possibly want to spend.

Then came Hurricane Katrina.

He had been thinking of moving back for years. Texas pleased him, no doubt. Houston was the big city and he relished the fact that he had made it there, and on his own terms. But for a boy born and raised on the smell of chicory and jambalaya, a part of him always missed the Crescent City. So at the moment when thousands of people were fleeing for their lives, Tommy decided to leave his life in Houston and return to New Orleans.

His mother Luisa had been staying with him in Houston after her air conditioner in New Orleans had given out for the umpteenth and final time. Together they watched Katrina's devastation unfold on the news, checking in by any means possible to make sure friends and relatives were safe from harm. Tommy grew up perfectly, happily middle class in The Marigny, a neighborhood not wealthy but by no means poor. Their home was a Quarter-adjacent, three-bedroom cottage on half an acre, surrounded by magnolia and oak trees that had been there for decades. Only the trees and their garage with an apartment above were left habitable after Katrina.

This was Tommy's opportunity to move back. He wanted to help rebuild. At first it was all manual labor, digging and cleaning. The work was hard but Tommy loved it. Being outdoors rejuvenated him. Soon Tommy realized he was reconnecting with the community, asking about old friends, and seeing people he hadn't seen in years. Tales of years past led to talk of the present, mourning the dead, families displaced, the lawsuits—endless lawsuits. . . .

It dawned on Tommy that there were countless people who were too poor to procure decent legal representation. He loved the law and loved trying lawsuits. Thus, the Riley Law Group was born—Tommy's own strictly pro-bono law firm.

He'd even made a fortune off the hurricane itself by way of property. In the messy aftermath, when United States congressmen were casting aspersions on the city's ability to bounce back, people were selling property for pennies on the dollar. He hadn't intended to hold onto the old house in The Marigny and wait out the market. He hadn't really thought about it.

But he was the son of local legend Paddy Riley. People knew the tall, handsome guy with mud up to his armpits, cleaning out abandoned buildings that reeked of death and despair, had made a fortune in Houston. And they reached out. Soon Tommy owned almost one-square mile of property, stretching all the way to the Bywater.

The Big Easy bounced back in a big way. Neighborhoods that had been considered unsafe before Katrina were now home to the trendiest, most-gentrified establishments in the state. His family's old house had been turned into a farm-to-table restaurant where Tommy was welcomed back weekly with warm hugs and the best gumbo in the city. He'd been given a golden ticket and was eager to give back. And as he drove to his office on this beautiful September day in New Orleans, Tommy felt a surge of contentment.

He wheeled the big Navigator into the parking lot adjacent to the three-story office building he had purchased and remodeled when he opened the firm. It was in downtown New Orleans just off Canal Street, in one of the brick low-rises that, on higher ground, had mostly survived Katrina. Its only tenants were the associate lawyers, paralegals, and support staff for the Riley Law Group. It was also conveniently located next to the St. Charles streetcar line. Most of the attorneys used Manuel to drive them around the city; he had worked for Tommy's dad years earlier. Tommy wouldn't chance Riley associates being late for court or mediation hearings because of a streetcar delay or a walk in a New Orleans rainstorm. But the streetcar was very convenient for their clients who, for the most part, had very little means.

Betty Lincoln, a cup of coffee in one hand and a file folder in the other, greeted Tommy with her ever-present radiant smile as he loped into the reception area. Betty was exceptionally pretty, even in advancing years. She wore her dark, curly hair in a neat, short bob with a few straggling strands of gray starting to sprout through. As Tommy's executive assistant and office administrator for the ten-lawyer firm, Betty was his first hire when he opened the firm. He had known her family for so long that he couldn't remember not knowing them.

"Good morning, boss," Betty said, still smiling at him as she took her seat behind her ornate desk facing the door. "You look chipper. What's wrong?"

"Why shouldn't I be?" he chimed back. "The Saints destroyed the Dolphins last week, I'm telling you, Betty—"

"Yeah, yeah, 'This is their year.' Now, where have I heard that before? Oh, I know. It was right here in this office. Last year. And the year before that. And the year before that. And the year before that," Betty teased.

"We'll always have 2009," Tommy said wistfully, the memories of the post-Katrina Super Bowl win still etched vividly in the city's collective consciousness.

"We most certainly will," said Betty. "Ain't no one ever gonna take that away."

"I want you to get me two tickets for tonight's game. Fifty-yard line."

Betty smiled, "Fifty-yard line. Will Ms. Butler be joining you?"

"Doubtful. She's in court tomorrow."

Betty rolled her eyes, "Two tickets huh? Who's the lucky guest?"

Tommy glanced at his Omega. "It's only nine. Gimme until lunch." Tommy smiled. "So what's on the docket?"

"Silk wants to meet with you about a potential new client he talked to yesterday afternoon. You have a meeting with Alejandra Batista. And Gerald wants you to review an appellate brief before he files it. It's due today."

"Who is Alejandra Batista?" Tommy inquired.

"Don Stoop at the ACLU referred her. My guess is she went to him first but her situation didn't fit the charter. She asked to speak to you specifically."

"Lucky me." As he trotted into his office, he said, "Hey, maybe she likes football."

CHAPTER FOUR

Tommy was engrossed in the appellate brief and making notes in the margin when Betty rang in.

"Ms. Batista is here to see you."

"Thank you, Betty," he said.

Stepping out into the lobby, Tommy was immediately struck by the wholesome and earthy woman rising from the couch to greet him. She was maybe five feet six inches tall with thick, shiny, raven hair. No makeup and piercing amber eyes that put him immediately at a loss. Tommy prided himself on being an unfailing judge of character. But this woman seemed a cipher upon introductions. And something told him not to underestimate her based on her unadorned appearance.

He said, smiling, "Tommy Riley," and shook her hand.

She responded with a firm grip. And finally, a smile as bright as her eyes. "Mr. Riley, I'm Alejandra Batista."

Tommy relaxed. He had a feeling he'd take her case, whatever it was. *But let's not get ahead of ourselves,* he thought.

As he led Alejandra into his office, asking her to sit down, Tommy noted the cream-colored dress that could not conceal the woman's trim, athletic figure. He was a consummate professional, always. But he was also a man and the two often fought for dominance in any given situation when an attractive woman walked into his office.

In a city with the temptations of New Orleans, with endless wealth and opportunity, Tommy had instituted a series of rules of self-discipline. One of them he called his "daughter rule." Simply put, he would never date anyone twenty years his junior, making her young enough to be his daughter if he had one. In his thirties, his daughter rule had never been an issue, but it had become more problematic in his forties. He thought Alejandra Batista would be off limits, but just barely. It was for the best, really. It was good to put those thoughts aside right off the bat.

After she declined water and coffee, Tommy asked her, "How may I help you, Ms. Batista? Is it Miss? Mrs.? Ms.? Dr.? Professor? What titles am I forgetting?"

She laughed. "Ms. is perfectly correct modern terminology. I'm not married. Are you married, Mr. Riley? You can call me Allie by the way."

"No, no I'm not," he answered.

"Have you ever been married, Mr. Riley?" she asked.

"No, I haven't. Not yet I guess. Maybe someday," he said.

"Are you Catholic, Mr. Riley?"

"Straight to religion. Bold follow-up, Ms. Batista," Tommy answered.

"It's relevant to my case," she replied, seeming to tighten up slightly. "I'm trying to decide whether to engage your services."

Tommy wanted to put her at ease, lowering his voice. "First of all, relax. We're good people here, religious or not. But no one engages this firm. All the work we do for our clients is pro bono. We only win if you win. And quite frankly, Ms. Batista, I don't need any more money than I already have. So I only take cases that I personally believe in."

Alejandra looked at him for a moment. "You don't need any more money."

"Nope."

"And you call yourself a lawyer," she grinned.

Tommy laughed. Alejandra has a sense of humor, he thought. Relieved.

"May I ask you another question?" she asked.

Riley nodded his head. "Shoot."

"It's going to sound familiar. Are you Catholic? With an Irish name, I think you might be," she said.

"Yes. My parents are both Catholic. My father is deceased, but my mother, an Italian-American, is still with us. I'm Catholic by default, I suppose. Altar boy when I was a kid. The whole bit."

"Are you a practicing Catholic, Mr. Riley?" she continued.

"Does one midnight Mass every five years count? No, not any more. Ms. Batista, clearly religion has something to do with your case, so why don't you tell me—"

"The Catholic Church specifically. I want to sue the Catholic Church." She thought for a moment. "I am going to sue the Catholic Church."

Tommy took a moment to study her face. He thought he knew where this was going and wanted to cut the discussion short.

"Ms. Batista, this firm, as a matter of principle, does not represent victims of pedophilia by Catholic priests. And before you ask, it has nothing to do with my religion. Somebody reads that a priest he or she knew in their youth has been accused of molestation, they see it as an opportunity. I'm not saying that's you. But it happens. It's ugly. And it's an area of litigation that we stay away from."

"I'm not here because I had a sexual encounter with a priest, Mr. Riley," she said determinedly.

“Then what has the Catholic Church done to you that is grounds for a lawsuit?” Tommy asked.

“Mr. Riley, I’m here because I need you to represent me,” she said determinedly. “I want to sue the Catholic Church to allow me to enter the seminary. I want to become a priest.”

CHAPTER FIVE

Tommy was seldom at a loss for words but he sat frozen, locked into Alejandra's unwavering amber eyes and finally stammered, "Ms. Batista—"

She tried to take the tension out of the moment, demurely replying, "Please, call me Allie."

He knew she was playing him like a harp, but at the same time he was fascinated by what she might do to a jury.

"Only if you call me Tommy," Riley replied.

"I prefer to call you Mr. Riley, if that's okay."

"You make the rules, Allie. Clearly." Tommy leaned back in his chair. "So you want to take on the Catholic Church to overturn a 2,000-year-old doctrine—believed to be the Word of God, by the way—that bars women from the clergy. Just so we're clear."

"The laws of this country prevent unjust discrimination against women based solely upon their gender. I am a woman in this country. The Catholic Church is an institution subject to the laws of this country. Is it not required to abide by the law?" she asked heatedly.

"Sure. But the First Amendment also clearly defines a separation between church and state. That precludes United

States laws from intervening into the activities of a church. A church has the right to practice its religion as it chooses."

"I understand," Allie responded. "But the same Constitution also requires the separation between the branches of the government. Yet in the last forty years, there has been a president that was forced to resign because he violated laws enacted by the legislature and another president that was impeached by the legislative branch. The judicial branch just blocked the executive branch from violating that same Constitution. If the president of the United States is not exempt from the laws of this country, how can any church be exempt? And when Florida required a controversial re-count during the 2000 election, the Supreme Court, the highest institution of the judicial branch, inserted itself into the legislative process. In this country, it's clear that the law and the courts established to enforce that law are paramount over the separation of the executive, legislative, and judicial branches. How can the Church hide behind the separation of church and state when their actions are likewise clearly a violation of United States law?"

Tommy was impressed. He grinned and said, "You sure you wouldn't rather be a lawyer?" He turned serious. "I'll send you to law school and hire you here. And I'm not even joking. It will be cheaper, easier, and probably quicker than what you're proposing."

Allie became quiet and her eyes fixed on his with an unnerving intensity. "God has called me, Mr. Riley. God has called me, not as a woman but as a person. I intend to answer that call. It's that simple," she said.

Tommy let out a protracted sigh. He took out a legal pad and pen and said, "Well then. Let's start at the beginning."

"I was born in Houston twenty-seven years ago," she began.

"Houston!" Tommy interrupted. "I miss the kolaches.

They have them here but—"

"They're the not the same," they said, in unison.

"Please continue," said Tommy.

"My father and mother were very religious Mexican Catholics, and raised me and my four brothers and three sisters in the Catholic Church. We attended Mass at St. Peter and Paul, and I went there to parochial school from kindergarten to the eighth grade. After that I went to St. Gwendolyn High School and graduated valedictorian of my class." Then she grinned and said, "But since it is an all-girls' school, and I didn't compete against any boys, maybe you're not so impressed."

Tommy looked up at her smiling face and said, "Impressive nonetheless. Please continue."

"I received an academic scholarship from Loyola University, the Jesuit school here, and earned an undergraduate degree in theology and a doctorate in Trinity Studies," she continued.

Tommy looked up with a grin. "There are boys at Loyola. Did you graduate valedictorian there?"

"Yes, I did," she said, with a confidence that Tommy admired.

He chuckled with embarrassment. "Touché."

Allie continued, "The faith that my parents instilled in me is the core of my life. I serve at St. Mary of the Angels where I work with children."

Tommy looked up. "That church is by my old neighborhood. So Ms. Batista, you're a Sister? I mean, Sister, you're a nun?"

Allie laughed, "I told you to call me Allie."

As soon as Tommy blurted, "You just don't see Sisters that look . . ." He regretted it and tried to recover. "That wear . . ." He pointed at her dress and gave up.

"We don't all look like Whoopi Goldberg in Sister Act,"

she exclaimed with both hands at once in a way Tommy found attractive. And then she winked.

Tommy thought, *This lady would absolutely destroy a jury.*

"I also teach religion at Loyola. I spend my free time reading the Bible and books of Christian scholars," she said. "Mr. Riley, I have prayed for years over this decision, and God has given me His answer. In my heart, and in my mind, I know he wants me to be a priest. And he has led me to you for help. I'm an excellent candidate for the priesthood, as qualified or more so than any man who applies. The only thing—and I mean the only thing—I don't have in the way of qualifications in the Church's eyes is a Y chromosome. Male genitalia. Why is the presence of a penis a fundamental requirement for a celibate priesthood?"

Tommy shrugged, "Good question."

"All priests take a vow of celibacy when they enter the priesthood. Since a priest may not have sex, what does a priest's sex have to do with it? If I had an operation and changed my gender, would the Church say I'm more qualified than I am now?"

"Have you considered that?" Tommy asked.

"Considered what?" Allie answered.

"We've represented a number of transgender people in court. You might have a better chance on those grounds."

"But don't you see how ludicrous that is?" Allie pleaded.

"I do," he responded.

Tommy stared at Allie. This woman was honest and endearing, and he was impressed by her zeal. She would be appealing in a courtroom. She was appealing now. But it was time to dig in.

Tommy cleared his throat and said, "Allie, have you thought about what will happen if you file a lawsuit against the Catholic Church? The church has enormous resources, maybe more than any other institution in the world. They will overturn every aspect of your life. Your parents, your family, your friends will all be involved. Are you ready for that? Are you ready for all those you love, their lives and their relationships, to be put under a microscope? The church will try to find out everything they can to show that you are neither passionate nor serious about what you want." Tommy paused here before continuing.

"If you are a private person, and I suspect you are, prepare yourself for a firestorm of condemnation by media. They will also dig to find any dirt they can. Expect to see some kid you barely knew on cable news telling the whole world you were the greatest lay he ever had. It'll be a lie, but no one will care. You could sue for slander, but what good would that do? Make no mistake, Allie, this'll be a lawsuit that the Church cannot afford to lose. And when the Catholic Church can't afford to lose, they don't lose. The best you can hope for is some sort of settlement with an airtight NDA after years and years of harassment. You'll never be able to tell anyone what you went through."

"I'm not afraid, Mr. Riley. Are you?"

Tommy dropped the notepad to the desk and rubbed his eyes. He had thought he would be more hesitant than he was. "I want to do some research, see if we have a leg to stand on. Give me the weekend?"

Allie grabbed the notepad and began writing. "Here is my address and number. I live with two other nuns. They are very good friends."

"And have you talked to these two nun friends about your decision?" Tommy inquired.

"Sister Mary Caroline heartily supports me. Sister Josephine . . . is having a tougher time with it," she answered.

Tommy rose from the couch, chuckling and said, "Your first opinion poll. Get used to it."

They stood together for a moment. "Goodbye, Allie. You've given me a lot to chew on."

As he extended his hand to say goodbye, she looked deep into his eyes and said, "Thank you, Mr. Riley. You're not alone in your decision, you know." Then she turned and gazed outside. Slowly she turned back to face him and said with quiet intensity, "God will be with you every step of the way. Whatever decision you make will be the right one." With that, Tommy escorted Allie to the door and she left.

Her absolute conviction in God was overpowering. Tommy wondered if he could ever have a belief about anything the way she did.

CHAPTER SIX

As Tommy walked back into the reception area, Betty was at her desk with a Cheshire cat grin.

"God's hands?" she asked, stifling a giggle.

"First time for everything," he replied with a distance uncharacteristic to his usual demeanor.

"Uh oh," she said. "She really got to you, this Alejandra Batista."

"Did you get those tickets?"

"Pretty lady. Pretty Sister lady."

"Betty."

"Signed, sealed, and delivered into my competent and elegant hands."

As Tommy headed back to his office, he called back, "Give them to Leroy and Benjamin."

Leroy was Betty's husband. Benjamin was their youngest child, a junior in high school. The older two children had left for college. Leroy was the total opposite of Betty in physical appearance. Betty's income more than provided a comfortable lifestyle, so Leroy took on the role of homemaker. A truly modern arrangement that suited them well. And one thing was for certain—Betty and Leroy were a very happily married couple.

As Tommy stepped back into his office, Betty rang the intercom.

"What makes you think that Leroy and Benjamin would want to waste their time watching the A'ints?" she asked. Betty had been around long enough to remember the days when Saints fans attended games with paper bags over their heads.

"They might enjoy a night away from you," Tommy replied.

"Hmmm. Okay, I'll take them home and they can have them if they want. Assuming the dog doesn't eat them first."

In spite of himself, Tommy smiled. "Okay, now that that's settled, I need to speak to Silk."

CHAPTER SEVEN

Willis Thompson had been "Silk" since college. At his first day of basketball practice at the University of Texas, Willis went to his right on the dribble and left the senior guarding him stuck to the floor with a cross-over move that seemed like he'd teleported to the basket. Rather than slam the ball home, he calmly laid the ball in, not wanting to embarrass an upper classman. The Texas coach merely said, "That was smooth as silk. Yessiree Bob, smooth as silk."

When Silk walked into Tommy's office, he noticed Tommy was staring out the window. He stood there for a moment, and when Tommy didn't turn around, Willis cleared his throat, breaking Tommy's reverie.

"Sorry, Silk. Lost in thought there for a second," Tommy said.

"Anything to do with that fantastic looking young lady who just left?" Willis replied.

Tommy continued, "Her name is Alejandra Batista. She's a nun and she wants to sue the Catholic Church."

"I thought we were staying away from sexual abuse cases. Guess it didn't hurt her faith none."

"She is not hurting in the faith department. And it's different.

She wasn't molested. She wants to become a priest," Tommy replied.

There was silence for a long moment as Willis stared at Tommy. Finally, Willis chuckled, "Well, that is different."

Tommy thought a moment and then said, "Contact Tim Prentice and see if he can start an immediate investigation on Ms. Batista." Tim Prentice, a former FBI agent, was the best private investigator in New Orleans and had a very proficient team who uncovered the secret life that Tommy felt most, if not all, people had.

Silk responded, "I'll get him started first thing Monday morning. Big game tonight."

Silk was the smartest person Tommy had ever met. He was so smart that he sometimes forgot that mere mortals required time to do things.

"I had tickets. But I'm working. He needs to start yesterday. And it needs to be done by Monday morning."

"Got it," Silk turned to leave. "Hey, since you're not using those tickets—"

"You can wrestle Betty for them, if you like."

Silk just smiled "No, I'm good. Looks better on the 60 inch anyway."

Tommy reviewed the notes he took during his conversation with Allie, which included her social security number, the schools she attended, present and former addresses, and the like. "This will get him started. Tell him to approach this as if she were a witness in a crucial case in which we'd have to cross-examine about her lifestyle. Also talk to Danielle Sullivan and Randi Bush," Tommy said.

Danielle and Randi were female lawyers who joined the firm after graduating in the top 10 percent of their law-school classes. The firm afforded them the flexible hours to be married, raise a family, and still utilize their expertise in legal research. In today's digital legal world, Danielle and Randi were equally effective at home or at the office.

"Have them research the issues for a case like this. The Catholic Church has the First Amendment. On the other hand, the Civil Rights Act of 1964 prohibits discrimination of women without justifiable cause for employment. Now, the act specifically excludes churches and their employees. But that was 1964. And I know there have been court cases that have expanded the rights of women since. Have Danielle and Randi get together to divide areas of research. I want to know if the United States District Court, Eastern District of Louisiana, has appropriate jurisdiction and venue to hear this case. And I want to know if we can even get this case to a jury."

"And you need this—" Silk felt his Thursday night slowly slipping away. Tommy just stared back.

Silk answered his own question. "Guess I can always record it."

Tommy and Silk didn't know each other back in high school, but they certainly knew of each other. As star athletes at the largest Catholic and public schools, respectively, they had faced each other as opponents dozens of times. Once they found themselves both freshmen on scholarships inside the massive University of Texas athletic department, they had bonded as only New Orleanians can.

Tommy was completely comfortable turning all the legal research over to Silk. While playing basketball at UT, Silk had graduated in three years with a 4.0 average in History, with a minor in African American studies. With one year of athletic eligibility left, he had taken the LSAT and passed with flying colors. He enrolled in UT law school as a first-year student while playing his senior year of basketball, a feat nobody could remember having been accomplished at Texas before. Two years later, he had graduated first in a class of 282. Now both back home in New Orleans, he was Tommy's indispensable go-to guy and best friend.

"We're not really gonna take this on?"

Tommy didn't answer.

Silk smiled. "I might have to interview her. Might have to find out what is going on in that pretty little head."

Tommy laughed out loud. Silk had more offers than Tommy, even though he was happily married to the same lovely woman since college. Tommy was mostly a scrub at the collegiate level, barely staying on scholarship. Willis "Silk" Thompson was a bona fide star, the kid who turned down the NBA to become a lawyer, and never regretted it. But he sure did love to talk a good game.

"Silk, you're married. And she's a nun. And also, you're still married. And she's still a nun."

Silk feigned annoyance. "Tommy, when you go on all your trips to Paris, when you go to the Louvre, do you touch the paintings?"

Tommy had heard it before but it always amused him. "No, Silk, you get in trouble if you touch the paintings."

"Exactly! I don't want to touch the Mona Lisa. I just want to look at it."

"Silk, one of these days . . ." Tommy knew that Silk could double his salary working at one of the big firms in town. But he also understood that Silk hated the very messy business of big law. So he paid Silk five times what a top pro-bono lawyer would normally make. New Orleans was proud of their hometown hero that had been a star at UT, so the good-will and publicity that Silk engendered within the community was priceless.

"Fine, fine. Let me just ask you then. Is she for real?" Willis asked.

"I think so, Silk. I really do. But let's see what Tim and his nerds find out," Tommy said.

As Willis reached the door, Tommy said, "By the way, did you know a recent poll said that Catholic nuns were split down the middle on whether women should be priests?"

"I didn't know that," Willis said, turning around. "Is that relevant?"

"Not really," Tommy answered. "But I was just thinking, Joe Bob would take fifty-fifty anytime."

CHAPTER EIGHT

Tommy spent the rest of the day taking calls, talking to associates, reading briefs, and taking care of various tasks that the head of the leading pro-bono firm in the largest city in Louisiana would deal with. The organizations that referred clients to the Riley Law Group were numerous. They included every charity in New Orleans—the ACLU, Alcoholics Anonymous, Al-Anon, Aliteen, and Planned Parenthood. It made for a varied and wildly exciting legal life.

He was relieved when the workday was over. He left the office, climbed into his Navigator, and drove to his home in the Warehouse District. Tommy loved the Garden District, site of elegant plantation-style homes and massive oak trees, and had since he was a child. He always figured he'd move there when he got older, got married, or became wealthy. Now that he was the latter, he still felt too young and too single to move to that most genteel part of town. He felt comfortable in the luxury, low-rise Tchoupitoulas Tower; close to work, close to his favorite blues bars and cocktail lounges, and refreshingly far from his high-school friends who all lived Uptown. He tossed the keys to the porter and took the elevator to his apartment.

Tommy didn't mind drinking alone, or even attending the occasional movie by himself, but he disliked eating alone in public. If he sat at the bar it was one interruption after another; if he requested a table, well, that was just awkward.

Tommy changed into shorts and a Saints t-shirt and went into his kitchen. He took out a prime New York strip steak, one from a shipment he had regularly sent in from the Wooden Nickel in Crested Butte. While it marinated, he sliced a potato into wedges, seasoned them, and put a head of lettuce in the freezer. He flipped on the game just in time for kickoff.

He grabbed a bottle of Bushmills Irish Whiskey from the vintage mahogany and etched-glass liquor cabinet, and regarded the label with a smile. His father had been a Jameson's man, the Catholic whiskey. So naturally Tommy chose Bushmills, the whiskey of the Protestant British North, before he was old enough to drive. Even at an early age, it was his own slyly transgressive achievement, or what passed for rebellion in an otherwise happy and relatively normal childhood.

Whether early in the morning or late at night, Tommy had never seen his mother Luisa turn down a glass of red wine. But whiskey to her was the devil's elixir, and when she found Tommy at aged 14 drinking Bushmills—neat no less—she had a conniption that would raise the dead. Tommy smiled whenever he thought about that day. Luisa was no stranger to the belt, but the big punishments she left to Paddy. When he came home for supper before another stint at the bar, Luisa silently deposited the bottle on the dinner table with a nod to the boy. She retreated to the kitchen, her sanctuary, awaiting the sounds of hellfire and redemption. What she heard, to her dismay, was laughter.

"Bushmills, eh?" his father had asked as Tommy nodded glumly. "It's a shite whiskey, no wonder you couldn't finish."

Paddy stared sternly into the boy's eyes as he slowly unscrewed the cap. He took a very long swig, then looked quizzically at the bottle. "It's not half bad, you know. Tastes very much like Jamie, in point of fact." He pointed to the top of his head. "Do you see anything? Growing up there?" Tommy shook his head. "They told us we'd grow horns if we drank the whiskey of the north. I guess they were mistaken." There is a moment in every boy's life when he crawls out from behind his mother's apron and begins to see his father as a real human being. Tommy allowed himself the slightest grin. Paddy pushed the bottle forward. "Your turn then."

Tommy's mind snapped back to the present. He poured a healthy amount of Bushmills Black Bush into a tumbler over ice. He took a Cusano, an eighteen-year-old, double-wrapped Connecticut cigar from his humidor and went outside. It was a beautiful night. His apartment had terraces on all four sides, and he chose the one facing south. Lights stretched out along the black, seemingly endless Gulf of Mexico. As he clipped his cigar, lit it, and took a sip of Black Bush, he pondered the fate of Alejandra Batista.

After his second Bushmills, Tommy went into the kitchen and pulled a bottle of Titus Cabernet, opening and decanting it. He put the potatoes in the oven, the steak on the indoor grill, and pulled the lettuce out to cut into a wedge. This was his nightly ritual.

The Saints were down 28-7 at the end of the first half. Tommy switched the TV off.

After dinner, Tommy retired to the living room with a glass of wine and reflected. If Allie was right and whatever decision he was going to make over the weekend was in God's hands, he sure wished God would hurry up about it. It was barely nine o'clock and, as per usual, he felt restless.

He picked up his phone. Tommy was committed to never having Manuel drive him anywhere on a Sunday. But as for the rest of the week? He was on a full salary and worked an average of four hours a day. From the other end, "Hey Mr. Riley! Can you believe this game? We've got no defense."

Moments later, Manuel was driving Tommy to the French Quarter. Tommy was a regular at several of New Orleans' classier drinking dens. As with so many other aspects of his life, Tommy adhered to a few simple rules to make sure he didn't give in to the temptations of the Big Easy. The first was to divide the city into neighborhoods, then allow himself only one bar per neighborhood. That way he could be a regular without being a carouser.

In the French Quarter, he had chosen the Carousel Bar at the Hotel Monteleone. It was elegant and in a prime location—the perfect place to treat important out of town visitors. He could close a deal by the end of happy hour, then send his associates on their merry way. Mostly it was quiet, or at least quieter. Tommy had been on so many first dates there he couldn't count that high, which was a secret that he and the bartender, Terry Stevens, never divulged.

Tommy wondered, as he often did, if he drank too much. He had never thought of his father Paddy as an alcoholic, but the poor man was not yet 60 when he died of liver failure.

"Terry," he asked, "what is the definition of an alcoholic?"

Terry thought about it before responding. "An alcoholic can go weeks without a drink, but once they start, they can't stop until they are totally inebriated. That said, the best test is to drink two drinks a day—no more, no less—for thirty days. If a person can do that, it's highly unlikely they're an alcoholic."

"I don't know. I don't get drunk. But I drink more than two every day," Tommy replied. "Can I count a full glass of Bushmills as a single drink?"

Terry laughed and thought a minute, then said, "Maybe you're a functioning alcoholic."

Tommy seemed glum. "Beats the alternative, I guess."

Terry knew him better than that. "Tommy, you grew up in a bar. Your tolerance is through the roof. How old were you when you had your first sip of beer?"

Now it was Tommy's turn to laugh. "Eight or nine? I used to sip the empties when I took them back to the kitchen."

"That's disgusting, you know that?" Terry slid over an empty that had been sitting on the bar. "On the house."

Tommy laughed again. "Disgusting is right. Then I was refilling Jack Daniel's bottles with the cheap stuff by the time I was 12. Never did get caught."

Terry pointed to his eye. "That's what you think. Your old man knew everything. He didn't whip you because you were saving him money. Plausible deniability."

"It's a wonder I'm still alive, when you think about it."

"Look, Tommy, if you had a problem, you'd know it by now. This is New Orleans. I'm your bartender, your confessor, and your friend. If you start to slip, I'll let you know. And on that note, have a double. It's on me."

CHAPTER NINE

On Saturday morning, Tommy rode his bike to the New Orleans Rowing Club on Bayou St. John, then rowed all out for 30 minutes, showered, and changed. It was time for his visit with his mother. He had been born the only child of Patrick Thomas Riley and Luisa Maria (née Risso) Riley and christened Thomas Patrick; he had the good fortune of receiving the best genes of his Irish father and his Italian mother. Paddy was an outgoing fellow whom everyone knew, always armed with a good story and a hearty laugh. As a natural result of his bubbly personality and a genuine affection for Irish whiskey and Guinness stout, Paddy had owned a pub. Paddy's, the only appropriate name for such an establishment, was a popular spot on Toulouse Street in the heart of the French Quarter.

The pub was a good business, and Paddy always generated enough income that Luisa and Tommy never wanted for anything. The downside was that Paddy felt compelled to be at the pub from the time it opened until closing. It was open 363 days a year, the only exceptions being Christmas and Easter, as demanded by Luisa. But even on Easter Sunday, there was often a steady procession of regulars drinking until all hours after a stern Easter Mass. That did not allow for much family time, and Tommy did not see much of his father during his childhood years. So Luisa took up the slack.

Paddy had been born and raised a Catholic, but he treated Catholicism like the other things he had been born with. He simply accepted his Catholicism like he accepted that he had red hair, blue eyes, and a tall, fit build. There was nothing Paddy could do about any of them, and certainly nothing to get excited over. Luisa, on the other hand, felt deeply connected to her Italian heritage and Catholic religion—and she did her utmost to share her feelings with the two men in her life. Since Paddy was not around much, her efforts were focused on Tommy. She made sure he attended daily Mass and enrolled him in a local, parochial school. He was expected to be an altar boy and to follow all the rules. In high school, Luisa had insisted that Tommy enroll in De La Salle High School, one of only two co-educational Catholic high schools in New Orleans.

Upon graduation, Tommy accepted a football scholarship to the University of Texas. Paddy was justifiably proud; Luisa was not. She wanted her son to attend Loyola University New Orleans, a well-regarded Jesuit school. She wanted him to continue his Catholic education in hopes that it would eventually lead to a religious vocation. For the first time since his maiden bottle of Bushmills, Tommy did not follow his mother's wishes. It had been another defining moment because Tommy had felt no guilt.

After Paddy died, Luisa remained in the house they had lived in for so many years. After Katrina, Luisa extended her temporary stay at Tommy's place in Houston. But she missed her parish and missed her friends, so once the city was back on its feet Tommy found space for her in an independent living center in the Garden District.

Luisa's new home was run by the Sisters of Mercy, who helped convince Luisa that it was a good option for her. A local priest said Mass daily and heard confessions regularly. Although Tommy would call on her periodically during the week, Saturday was the only day he had alone with his mother in person. And he cherished the special time with his mom.

Tommy called down for his roadster, a Panoz 1997 AIV. There were less than three hundred of them made. Its all-aluminum body with a handmade aluminum Cobra engine made it the fastest production automobile ever made in the United States at the time. His roadster didn't have a top, and it was a great spring day when Tommy roared out of Tchoupitoulas Tower.

When he arrived at the center, Luisa was waiting for him in the lobby. At 84, she was still a beautiful woman.

"Look at this elegant lady," Tommy said as he kissed her on the cheek. "You're the biggest heart-breaker the Sisters of Mercy have ever taken in."

Luisa smiled as she hugged him back. "Such blarney."

They both smiled at each other while momentarily lost in thoughts of Paddy. Tommy broke the silence and said, "It's a beautiful day, let's sit in the garden."

She agreed wholeheartedly, and they ventured outside into the sprawling, green sanctuary, Luisa with her walker and Tommy walking slowly beside her.

Tommy seemed somewhat preoccupied and Luisa noticed. "Something on your mind?" she asked.

"Just work stuff," Tommy answered. "Nothing to worry about."

"You've taken it home from the office. You never do that," Luisa replied.

"I have a potential new client with a very . . . interesting case," Tommy said.

Luisa looked at Tommy knowingly. "Want to talk about it?"

Tommy took a deep breath and finally said, "This woman wants to sue the Catholic Church to allow her to become a priest. She believes the laws against discrimination of women give her the right to require the Church to grant her admission to the seminary to study for the priesthood."

Luisa was silent for a long time. In a very even tone, she asked, "Do our laws give her that right? I find it hard to believe they do."

"We're looking into it."

Again there was silence. Then Luisa said, "Tommy, you've lived a charmed life. Things always come easy to you. When the knee injury ended your football career, the luck of the Irish led you to law school and Joe Bob. As a partner with Joe Bob, you received a great fortune. To your credit, you've used the money to do good things. But, Tommy, things have always come easy for you. You've never had to work for what you have achieved."

"Mom, first that's not true. But what does it have to do with—" Tommy was interrupted.

"Let me finish. You've avoided hard decisions all your life. That includes your personal life."

This conversation was going the way Tommy thought it would: not well. He knew his mother was disappointed that her only son had never married, never produced a grandchild. Time was running out. Tommy himself had been, for Luisa, a miracle. The child that couldn't be, arriving as she neared forty. It pained him greatly, so he smiled and said, "Mom, there's no other woman that can hold a candle to you."

"Don't give me the charm. This is a big decision, Tommy. Have you really thought about what's involved here?" Luisa said determinedly.

"Meaning?" Tommy asked.

"The Virgin Mary is the most revered of all saints. If the Catholic Church has a rule against women serving as priests, do you think it's out of disrespect to women, or do you think it's based upon a fundamental belief that such is the will of God?" Luisa answered.

"I think the Catholic Church has a doctrine based upon the teachings of Jesus. But when men in the Church begin to interpret those teachings, mistakes are made," Tommy answered.

"But you don't know that's the case in this instance, do you?" Luisa responded.

Tommy shrugged his shoulders and said, "If the physical attributes of a woman would not allow her to withstand the physical rigors that a particular job required, it would be legal to exclude her from consideration solely because of her gender. I don't see that being the case here. Frankly I don't know why the Church excludes women, so our legal system will compel them to make their case."

His mother touched his shoulder. "Tommy, you're good at what you do. I assume you would not file a lawsuit unless you thought you had a chance to succeed."

Tommy nodded.

"They say that an innocent act can have unintended consequences. All I ask is that you consider the negative consequences for the sixty-million practicing Catholics in the United States, including me," Luisa said.

Tommy studied her expression. What did she mean?

She continued, "If you were to win your lawsuit, you'll drastically change our religion forever. Do you really want to do this? Think of what you'd be doing to me."

"Mom, I love you, but this isn't about you. I'm not making any changes personally. If the Church changes something, it will be the rule of law that causes the change. We're a nation of laws. No person and no institution, including the Catholic Church, should be above the law."

She shook her head and said, "What about the laws of God, Tommy? What role does He play in your decision?" she asked.

"But why would you object, Mom? You've always been in favor of equality."

Luisa gave a long, hard stare at the son she raised, wondering who this stranger was next to her. "My son, equality has nothing to do with it."

With that, Luisa slowly got up out of her chair, positioned herself into her walker, and slowly retreated out of the garden into the main building without looking back. Tommy watched her go. He saw the conflict in his mother. She wanted to support him. But she was a Catholic and had dedicated her life to its tenets, including the one he might help overturn.

After a while, he got up to go himself. He walked through the lobby, said goodbye to the receptionist, then walked to his roadster in the parking lot. On a lonely country road along Lake Pontchartrain, Tommy jammed the gas pedal and felt the little roadster leap to eighty miles an hour. The wind felt good as it began to buffet his face.

CHAPTER TEN

Tommy had met Nikki Butler in a courtroom. Seven months earlier, Tommy was representing Danny Horton, a second-grade student in one of the local school districts. Both of Danny's parents were employed by a government contractor and stationed in Iraq. While they were overseas, the boy had lived with his maternal grandparents. Danny, in a show of love and honor to his parents, began wearing a wristband of red and blue with a white star in the middle. The school had demanded that Danny refrain from wearing the wristband. He refused to submit to the school's orders and was dismissed until such time that he would comply with the mandatory dress code. Danny's grandparents knew Betty Lincoln from church, enabling them to gain an immediate interview with Tommy. Without delay, he filed for an injunction in state district court to require the school to admit Danny to attend classes. Tommy won a temporary injunction, which allowed Danny to attend class pending the final determination. Since the county attorney had lost the first round, the school board decided to enlist the services of one of the premier law firms in New Orleans. Nikki Butler, a senior litigator at the firm, had drawn the case.

Nikki had argued forcefully that a uniform dress code was crucial in the public-school system to ensure orderly conduct. While the school district sympathized with Danny, deviating from the code of conduct could have detrimental consequences. If exceptions were made, then school-aged children might also wear paraphernalia designating gang affiliation, sexually-provocative dress, or sensitive slogans—all of which could spread disruption inside the classroom. Tommy had relied on the First Amendment and Danny's right to free speech. Though not entirely within the dress code of the school district, the wristband could not be considered provocative. Judge Van Horn had noticed that Danny was wearing Converse tennis shoes and asked whether they were within the dress code. When he was told they were, he suggested that perhaps red and white stripes could be tastefully painted on the shoes that already had the iconic blue star in the logo. The decision was readily accepted by all parties.

After the hearing, Nikki had approached Tommy and given him her card, on which she had written her cell phone number. A bemused Tommy called her thirty seconds later, as she walked to her car, and asked her to dinner. She laughed, immediately charmed by his moxie, and accepted. Seven months later, she was still charmed.

As Nikki walked through his front door that Saturday evening, anyone who saw the look on Tommy's face could tell he was positively smitten. She was tall and athletic, about five feet eight inches, with silky blonde hair and striking indigo eyes. She was also intelligent, witty, and perfectly content to listen to Tommy whenever the two high-powered lawyers stayed up late talking their way through the world's problems.

Before she could even remove her coat, Tommy leaned in with a kiss.

"That's nice," she murmured.

"Remember what happened the first time you said that?" he asked back.

"Why do you think I keep saying it?" She smiled.

He smiled back and asked, "Low flyer on the rocks?"

She answered with her standard, "But of course."

As she settled in on the cushy leather sofa, Tommy poured a generous amount of The Famous Grouse scotch whiskey over ice in a large glass tumbler. He was already working on his first Black Bush.

"What's for dinner?" she asked.

"I thought we would have take-out," he answered.

She looked at him quizzically. "Since when is the great chef not interested in cooking?"

Tommy didn't respond.

Nikki knew something was wrong. "Is everything okay with your mother?"

"Mom's fine. She might be worried her son is on an express train to hell over a case he's considering, though," Tommy answered. "Let's take this outside."

He took their drinks and led her out to the terrace on the north side where there was a cool breeze. Without speaking they both sat down in chairs side by side, allowing them to take in the expansive view in front of them. It was another crisp and clear night, and the lights of the tall buildings of the medical center seemed close enough to touch. Beyond, the lights of the skyscrapers in downtown New Orleans seemed to melt into a flat carpet of light stretching north to the horizon. The blinking lights of the jumbo jets queuing up to land at the airport thirty miles away dotted the sky.

Tommy looked at her and said, "So, her name is Alejandra Batista." He went on to describe his interview with Allie, the research assignments he had given his lawyers and investigators to do over the weekend, and concluded with his disturbing visit with Luisa that morning.

"As you can see, I'm torn. I'm not sure it's a case we can win, but I also feel a legal obligation to pursue it," Tommy said.

"You're not obliged to take on any client," Nikki responded.

"True," Tommy thought for a minute. "But there's some-thing about this case . . ."

"Do you believe in God, Tommy?" she asked.

Tommy noticed both of their glasses were empty. Silently he stood up, took the glass from her hand, and refilled both drinks inside at the bar. Returning to the terrace, he handed Nikki her glass and again sat down beside her.

"Where were we?" he asked, still lost in thought.

Nikki chuckled. "You were just avoiding my question."

"I'm not avoiding the question. But the answer isn't simply yes or no. To respond properly, I need to give you an explanation so you can understand why I answer the way I do. For that, I also needed a drink."

"It's a wonder you don't drink in the courtroom," she teased.

"How do you know I don't?" he chided back.

"This should be good," she said.

"For me," Tommy began, "all the intangible aspects of life such as trust, respect, and belief must be learned. I don't take someone or something at face value. I'm guided by actions and facts. I was raised Catholic, and the core of Catholicism is the belief in God as a matter of faith. But as I got older, I decided that if God existed, there had to be proof. I'm a lawyer. I would believe if the facts proved an existence. If not, then I could not believe. I asked myself, 'Does science point toward or away from the existence of God?'"

He continued, "Until the twentieth century, scientists believed the universe was eternal and static. The universe had always existed and always would.

"Then two things happened. The first was Albert Einstein and the theory of relativity. The second was the Hubble telescope. Both proved the universe was not static but in a continual state of expansion. If something is expanding, then at some time in the past that something had to have been continually smaller and denser—to the point at the beginning, which is nothing. Atheists believe this, too, and explain it with the Big Bang theory. Unfortunately for them, the laws of science state that something cannot arrive out of nothing. Whatever was there at the Big Bang must have been created first, and whatever created it had to be beyond the bounds of scientific laws." Tommy noticed Nikki staring at him intently, with a bemused grin. "Am I boring you yet?"

Nikki laughed. "This week, I listened to an expert witness testify for twelve hours about the minutiae of boat-owner insurance fraud. This is like watching *The Bachelor* compared to that."

"Okay, then there's physics. There are thirty different fundamental principles of physics that must be present to enable the universe to exist. Even if just one was slightly out of balance, the universe could not exist. These parameters are so finely tuned that the possibility of the universe occurring by accident is one in twenty to the hundredth power, which is a number that most mathematicians agree is infinitesimal. Science would say that this physical balance could not have been caused randomly. Therefore, the only logical conclusion is that it was accomplished through design. Einstein said it best when he said, 'I am convinced that God does not play dice.'"

Nikki was always up for a stimulating debate. "Okay, Tommy, science leads you to the conclusion of intelligent design. Many people believe that. But it doesn't necessarily lead to God. You're applying human probability numbers to an event that happened in a vacuum. Everything we know today came out of that event, but at the time of the Big Bang there was a different reality. You're trying to retrofit fourteen billion years of evolution into your theory."

Tommy immediately answered, "No. Whatever power created the universe has to be, by definition, beyond time and space. Why would a power with such immense logic do something illogical? Where's the logic in creating the universe and leaving it alone?"

"Maybe that's the whole point. What if logic is a human construct?" Nikki posed the question sincerely.

Tommy appreciated her intellect immensely; he had never been able to spar with another woman the way he did with Nikki. He was also slightly annoyed that her courtroom instincts were taking over. "Permission to approach the bench?"

"You've got two minutes."

He leaned over to her slowly and gave her a peck on the lips. Then looking her straight in the eyes. "May I finish?"

"Permission to continue."

Tommy took a long swig of Bushmills, stood up, and began pacing, as he would in front of a jury.

"Throughout recorded history man has been in awe of that which he could sense but not understand. Since man was afraid of those things, he worshiped them: the moon, the stars, the tides, and the weather. Man has worshiped many gods throughout time, and many at the same time. There is only one religion that historically worshiped one single God, and that is the one found in Jewish scripture. The Hebrews had a god they could not see, feel, or otherwise perceive. But they believed it operated in a logical manner. The facts tell me there is an intelligent designer, one who by definition has to operate logically, and the creator found in Jewish scripture is the only one who does that."

"You believe in the Jewish God?" Nikki asked, dubiously. "So, are you a Christian?"

"This again requires an explanation," he answered.

"Of course it does," she said, smiling.

He smiled and said, "To be a Christian is to believe that Jesus of Nazareth lived, died, and rose from the dead. Now, historical evidence states that Jesus of Nazareth did exist. Jewish scriptures also frequently talk about a Messiah to come. Was Jesus of Nazareth the Messiah described in those texts? The answer is *yes*, and it is conclusive."

"How so?" she asked.

"Many of the prophecies in their scriptures were very specific about who the Messiah would be. He would be born in the tribe of Judah, the family of Jesse, in the house of David. He would be betrayed by a friend for thirty pieces of silver, and He would be crucified, even though crucifixion was unknown at the time of the prophecies. The prophecies also foretold that King Herod would sentence all Jewish males two years old and younger to death, and the Messiah and his family would flee to Egypt. There are many more, the last prophecy being four hundred years before the birth of Jesus of Nazareth."

He paused, took a sip of his Black Bush, then continued, "Some mathematicians took just eight of the prophecies and calculated the odds of one person fulfilling those specific prophecies. The odds are one out of ten to the seventeenth power. The same mathematicians took the total forty-eight prophecies that matched the life of Jesus of Nazareth, and determined the odds of that occurring are one in twenty to the one hundred and fifty-seventh power. As we know, the odds of anything over one in twenty to the hundredth power are infinitely improbable."

"So you believe Jesus lived and that He is the Messiah described in Jewish scriptures?" Nikki asked.

"Yes. A belief that is based on those facts," Tommy answered.

"But does that make him the Son of God?" Nikki asked.

"Only if He could do something that no person has ever done or could ever do."

"Like turn water into wine."

"Leading the witness. No, that was a parlor trick. I believe based on historical fact that Jesus rose from the dead. We know for certain from the record that He was crucified. Did the crucifixion lead to His death? The centurion in charge of any crucifixion was bound to ensure the death of the crucified before taking him down from the cross. Failure to do so would cause the centurion to lose his life. Therefore, the centurion took the matter quite seriously. This particular centurion stabbed a spear into his side, which historians believe was into His heart, ensuring His death. This set of events was incidentally prophesied in the Jewish scriptures and, again, before crucifixion was known. I believe the evidence would indicate beyond a reasonable doubt that Jesus was dead."

Tommy became more animated as he continued. "So, the question becomes, did He come back from that death? We have eyewitness testimony of more than five hundred people who saw Jesus after His death. He appeared alive to them in thirteen separate instances. Were they lying? Why would they? There is no rational reason for them to have said what they said except that they believe it to be true. All of them were ostracized by society. Most of them died horrible deaths, which they could have avoided by renouncing Jesus as the Messiah. Yet none of them did. They knew what they had seen and convinced thousands and thousands of that fact. What do you think the odds are of winning a case with five hundred eyewitnesses and not one witness who can say otherwise? That is powerful evidence."

Nikki looked at Tommy for a while and said, "So in summary, you have convinced yourself, as an elite lawyer might, that you can use the very human concept of logic to prove the existence of God?"

"In summary, I believe the facts prove that Jesus of Nazareth lived, that He was the Messiah prophesied in the Jewish scriptures, and that He died and rose from that death. I believe He is the Son of God."

"There are countless Christian faiths in existence today," Nikki began, "Why are you a Catholic?"

Tommy answered, "History tells us that it was the first and original church. If I can have the original of anything, why would I settle for a copy?"

Nikki raised an eyebrow. "Because it makes exercising your religion sound like, I don't know, buying a painting." Nikki thought for a moment. "Do you pray?"

"Of course not. It's not logical."

CHAPTER ELEVEN

Tommy noticed that their glasses were empty. "Do you want to order some take-out?"

Nikki exhaled a long breath. "How 'bout another drink?"

"You okay?" Tommy asked.

"Oh, I'm great," Nikki smiled as she looked out at the streetcar below. "In the seven months I've known you, this is the first time you've opened up to me like this," Nikki answered. "I want to revel in it."

He smiled, took her glass with his own, left the balcony, and went back in to the bar. He returned with two drinks and one of his eighteen-year-old Cusano cigars. He handed her the drink, lit his cigar, and leaned back in his chair. Nikki had many fine attributes, but one of his favorites was that she enjoyed the smell of a good cigar.

"It's your turn. What do you believe?" Tommy asked.

"Well . . . my parent were hippies. They were at Woodstock, and we burned incense and practiced yoga way before it was hip—which makes me a flower child, I suppose. They were Christian in their own way, of the *Jesus Christ Superstar* variety. They always said, 'Jesus was the ultimate hippie.' They encouraged the lessons of the Bible but let us choose our own faith. So far I haven't found one. I'm not sure one needs an organization to have a meaningful relationship with God."

"Interesting," he replied, seeming to consider something.

"Many times I heard my parents say, 'Jesus didn't need a church to teach love.' So one day I looked it up. The entire foundation of organized Christian religion is pretty flimsy. He said, 'Upon this rock I will build my church,' but He was talking about Peter."

"Petros. The first Pope."

She continued, "I assume you disagree with that. Although I know you don't believe everything the Catholic Church teaches."

"Of course not," Tommy responded firmly. "The Catholic Church has been wrong many times."

"Give me an example." Nikki enjoyed challenging Tommy.

Tommy smiled. "Okay, but very quick, I promise. Take the celibacy of the clergy. Christ didn't teach celibacy. Many of the apostles were married with children. In the early church years, we know that many priests, bishops, and even popes were married. There were several instances of lineal heirs to popes being ordained a pope. Centuries later, a change was made that prohibited a priest from marrying only after ordination. Then in the seventeenth century, the rule of celibacy as it is taught today was enacted and, more importantly, enforced.

"Many historians believe the rule was enacted not out of a desire to dissuade a cleric from temporal desires, but to avoid the practical effect of feudal laws which required the firstborn son to inherit the estates of the father. See, this would put the title to church land on which the priest/father lived in dispute after his death. The ban of marriage for a cleric rendered any such offspring of a cleric to be illegitimate, with no legal standing to inherit the estate of his priest/father. Get where this is going?"

"A tidy solution to difficult legal problems," Nikki replied. She took a sip of her scotch. "Okay, let's cut to the chase. Male priests. What is the Church's reasoning?" Nikki asked.

"I have to assume that the Church has a solid foundation from the scriptures for the rule—a scriptural direction that would offer justifiable cause to discriminate against women."

"So, basically a civil rights exemption signed by Jesus Christ," she added.

"Exactly," he responded. "I need to find it by Monday, if it exists."

The two sat, staring off to the distance, drinks in hand. Finally, Nikki broke the silence.

"This is a tradition that goes back over two thousand years, at the very least. In the meantime, tens of thousands of clerics have consecrated the practice. I'd be shocked if there's established case law. What if there is no pertinent scripture?"

"Then it would have to be a man-made rule that meets the legal definition of justifiable cause under the Civil Rights Act," Tommy responded.

After a moment, Tommy said quietly, "Otherwise . . . we might have a shot."

CHAPTER TWELVE

Tommy awoke Sunday morning and dispensed with his usual workout routine. Instead, he chose a light pair of casual khaki slacks, a dark-green, short-sleeved polo, a light-beige sleeveless sweater, and a well-worn pair of peanut-butter-colored, ostrich-skin boots. He drove to Our Lady of Faith Catholic Church. After the 7:30 a.m. Mass, he waited until he was the last to leave. After Father Damien had bid farewell to the final parishioner with a hearty handshake, Tommy approached.

"Father," he said, extending his hand.

"Tommy Riley," Father Damien greeted him warmly. "Been a while, my boy."

"I must be attending the Masses you don't officiate," Tommy replied, with a mischievous grin.

"Same excuse your father used to give me," Father Damien smiled. "I didn't believe him either."

Tommy reddened slightly. "Got a minute, Father?"

"For wayward Catholics? Always. Let me get these vestments off, and I'll meet you in the garden."

Father Damien had been at Our Lady of Faith parish since Tommy was ten years old. Father Damien had been newly ordained in his mid-30s when he first came to Our

Lady of Faith, so Tommy figured the priest was at least seventy. He had always been a slight, spry man. And he still had that same bounce in his step. His dark hair had given way to gray and had become thinner. Other than the wrinkles imposed by age, he still looked the same.

Tommy entered the garden, tucked in between the rectory and church. It was often used for cake sales, raffle ticket sales, and fundraiser events for the Church. Today it was empty and Tommy was thankful for that. Father Damien met him, dressed in his traditional black cassock. They sat down on park benches at the side of the garden, near the enormous rose bushes that were still in full bloom. They were across from each other, and Father took out a packet of Marlboro Reds from the pocket of his cassock. As long as Tommy could remember, Father Paul Damien had smoked Reds. He shook one out of the packet, put it to his lips, lit it, and inhaled deeply.

"I thought the Church frowned on priests smoking in front of parishioners," Tommy joked.

Father Damien laughed. "Parishioners attend Mass."

Tommy laughed back. "How do you like the Pastor Emeritus gig?" Tommy asked.

"It's a pretty good deal. Since us old folks tend to get up early, I get the early Mass every Sunday. That allows the younger priests to sleep in, which they like. Plus, they get the larger congregations at the later Masses to hear their words of wisdom in their homilies. Most of the older parishioners like the 7:30 a.m. Mass, so I get to see old friends such as you today. I don't know if most of the celebrants are here because they're old like me and get up early; or if they know I say the Mass and it seems like old times."

"I'm sure it's the latter, Father Damien. You're a fixture," Tommy said sincerely.

"You didn't come here to talk about me. What do you have on your mind, Tommy?"

"I want to know what the qualifications are for the priesthood," Tommy replied.

"We're not thinking about a career change, are we?" Father Damien chuckled. "You would probably meet the basic qualifications. But I suspect you might have a problem with the rules and obligations that follow. I assume you've heard about celibacy."

Tommy waved him off. "You know me too well Father. But I *would* like to discuss those qualifications. Professionally."

Puzzled, Father Damien asked, "May I know the reason for your curiosity?"

"To the extent I can do so under attorney-client privilege, I will tell you what I'm working on. But I would like to save it until the end. Just consider I have a hypothetical candidate for the priesthood."

"Fair enough," Father Damien answered. "The qualifications are very basic. To be a candidate for priesthood one must be an unmarried male, baptized, and confirmed in the Catholic religion."

"That's it?"

"That's it," Father Damien replied. He continued, "I told you that you would meet the basic qualifications. Now comes the hard part, the procedures that attempt to satisfy the intangible qualifications."

After a moment of reflection, he asked, "Does your hypothetical candidate want to be a member of an order, or a diocesan priest?"

"Are the procedures different?" Tommy asked.

"Yes. The qualifications are the same, but the procedures are often different. If it helps your hypothetical candidate, I'm most familiar with the procedures in the Archdiocese of New Orleans. Shall I proceed?" Father Damien asked.

Tommy nodded yes, and Father Damien stubbed out his cigarette, putting the butt into a pocket of his cassock. From the other pocket, he took out his cigarettes and lit another.

"The first step in the procedure involves the priests in the parish where the candidate resides. He will talk to one of the priests about his desire for a vocation, and the ball starts rolling from there. He will talk to other priests in the parish, and based upon what they know about him, including his spirituality, personality, and dedication toward the priesthood, they may or may not recommend him to the diocese. Only if the priests in the parish in which he lives recommend him will the application be considered." Father paused for a moment to enjoy his cigarette.

"At that point, several interviews will determine whether the candidate possesses the intangible qualities required for the priesthood. A love for the Catholic faith, generosity, the will to help other people, a personal relationship with God, a capacity and desire to learn, a healthy self-image, good social skills, and the ability to enjoy one's own company. The priesthood is a solitary life.

"Since the scandals of course, a new element has been added. Psychological profile, interviews with psychologists, psychiatrists, sometimes more than one. They gather objective data about the candidate, personality tendencies—I'm sure you understand. The church takes it very seriously."

Tommy made a mental note of the psychological interviews. "What happens with the results of the interviews and tests? Are they compiled in written form?"

"Oh, yes. The church is a stickler for documentation. The written results are submitted to the head of the diocese, or the order, depending."

Tommy interjected. "That would be a bishop or archbishop, correct?"

"Correct. The ultimate decision whether to accept the candidate lies with the bishop or archbishop. There is no such thing as an appeal," Father Damien concluded.

"Okay, Father, now let's assume my hypothetical candidate can pass all of the interviews with flying colors. Let's assume, further, that this candidate is outstanding in every respect but one."

"Which is . . . ?" Father Damien inquired.

Tommy realized as he considered the question that he would require hours of patient practice in front of the mirror before he could confidently make his point to a jury. But he wanted to keep it simple for Father Damien, a man he had known most of his life. He blurted out, "She's a woman."

CHAPTER THIRTEEN

Father Damien turned his head to look Tommy in the eyes. There was a long moment of silence, and the man Tommy had known for years had a puzzled look on his face he had never seen before.

"Tommy, that's just not possible. Church doctrine stipulates that only males can become priests. It's futile to even pursue it."

Tommy put his elbows on his knees and leaned forward. "I know the Catholic Church will have a valid reason for excluding women from the priesthood. I just want to know what those reasons are. Father Damien, I have known you most of my life. You've earned my trust and respect and that's why I'm asking. Whatever you say will likely make my decision for me."

Father Damien simply stared at the rose bushes and lit another cigarette.

"Okay, Tommy, here it is. In 2005, Pope John Paul II stated as a matter of faith and morals that the priesthood was reserved for men only. When a pope speaks on issues of faith and morals, the Church believes his word on that issue is infallible. That's where the discussion begins and ends."

"But, Father," Tommy replied, "the rule has existed for two thousand years. We didn't need the Pope to know that. I have to assume the scriptures themselves contain the edict, right?"

"Tommy, I'll answer your question but you're not going to like it. Less than twenty years ago a council of bishops met, researched, and reviewed that very question."

Father Damien thought for a moment and took a deep hit off his cigarette. He knew he was opening Pandora's Box, but without honesty why was he even in the priesthood?

"Their conclusion is that there are no direct teachings in the scriptures on that particular point," Father Damien answered.

Tommy took a moment to let it sink in. "Father, if there is no direct teaching from the scriptures, what could possibly be the basis?" Tommy asked.

"The fundamental basis is Jesus Christ did not name a woman to be one of His original apostles. The apostles were the first priests of the Catholic Church."

Father Damien took another pull from his cigarette, exhaled, and continued. "Jesus Christ was the son of God and came to earth to redeem us. He was very different from other males of that time. He treated women as equals. When He named the apostles, He could have chosen a woman if He so wished. Many pagan religions had priestesses at the time. To name a woman as an apostle wouldn't have been out of the ordinary. He could have chosen His own mother Mary and Mary Magdalene, but He chose not to do so. When the eleven apostles chose the replacement for Judas, they chose a man, not a woman. They knew the intent of Jesus as well as anyone. As the apostles began to ordain priests, there is no record of the ordination of a woman. Also, a priest is Christ's representative on earth. Christ was a man, not a woman. As God, He could have chosen to be a woman, but He did not."

"So, Father, in the absence of a scriptural directive, the Church in essence bases its reasoning on something that Christ did not do but could have done?" Tommy asked.

"Yes."

"That's it?" Tommy asked incredulously.

"2000 years ago, yes. Now you're looking at a tradition that's been hallowed by practice and consecrated by time."

Tommy sat for a moment, watching Father Damien smoke. He asked, "The twelve apostles were all Jewish, were they not?"

Father Damien nodded.

Tommy continued, "There were Gentiles among the followers of Jesus. He could have easily named a Gentile as an apostle. Does that fact mean that all priests today should be Jewish?"

"That may have been more of a practical matter," Father Damien answered, "more to do with the customs of the times than an intention to bar Gentiles from the priesthood."

"The same can be said of women," Tommy said bluntly. Father Damien looked at Tommy but said nothing.

Tommy continued, "What about homosexuals? To our knowledge, none of the apostles were homosexual. In fact, most were married with children. If I remember correctly, the only apostle who wasn't married was Paul. If Christ didn't ordain a homosexual, why are they not barred from the priesthood today?"

Father Damien shifted on the bench and Tommy thought he may have touched a nerve.

Father replied, "Historically the Church has not considered sexual orientation as a prerequisite of priesthood. Everyone, gay or straight, has biological desires; it's what you do about them that counts. However, with the recent scandals there has been some discussion that a homosexual is more likely to be a pedophile than a heterosexual, even though there is no proof of that at all. There has been some direction from Rome to not accept homosexuals to the seminary. However, the directions seem vague, and Rome has clarified that it is the ultimate decision of the bishops or the head of the order. I personally believe that regardless of sexual orientation, if a priest maintains his vow of celibacy, then his orientation shouldn't make a difference. I've known homosexual priests, quite a few actually, and they have been and are excellent priests in all senses of the word. There is nothing about the vocation which requires a particular sexual orientation."

Tommy thought but did not say, *and gender identity is any different*?

Tommy worked over the new information in his mind and found a summation. "Jesus did not name Gentiles as priests, yet all priests today are Gentiles. Jesus did not name women or homosexuals as priests, but the Church today allows one and not the other. Does any of this make sense to you, Father?" Tommy inquired.

"It doesn't matter. The church is not a democracy, Tommy," Father Damien said.

"But this decision that affects the lives of hundreds of millions of women has been made by one man, Father, one man only—the Pope. Are you okay with that?" Tommy asked.

Father Damien rose from the bench and walked over to one of the rose bushes, handling a flower delicately.

"So this woman wants to become a Catholic priest," Father Damien said finally. "She wouldn't happen to be a religious sister in this archdiocese, would she?"

Tommy had figured that Allie's outspoken tenacity about her calling would not make her much of a secret amongst her peers. He sighed and replied, "I can't answer that."

The priest turned back to Tommy.

"A decision made by one man affects the lives of hundreds of millions of people. Am I okay with that? On matters of faith and morals in the Catholic Church, as an ordained priest in the Catholic Church, I'm okay with the pope making that decision. I'm not okay with you or a judge or your client making that decision, Tommy. I'm not okay with that at all."

With that, Father Damien walked slowly to the rectory without shaking hands or saying goodbye.

CHAPTER FOURTEEN

On Monday morning, Tommy arrived at the office and headed right for the conference room, a renewed purpose in his stride. Betty padded alongside him, taking his coat.

"Morning, boss. Scuttlebutt around here has it that you're out to get us all struck by lightning," Betty drawled.

Tommy replied dryly, "I wouldn't be shocked."

Betty groaned and said, "Comedy is not in your future, boss." Betty put on her all-business voice as they reached the conference room door. "The team is waiting for you, sir."

"Any chance there's beignets waiting for me too?" Tommy asked.

"What do you think?" Betty replied over her shoulder as she moved back toward the lobby.

Tommy called out, "You're the best."

"Mm-hmm," she said.

The team was already amid a heated discussion as Tommy entered the conference room, set down his briefcase, and poured a cup of coffee. He chose a beignet and stuffed it into his mouth.

"Who wants to begin?" Tommy asked with a mouthful of pastry.

Tim Prentice started reading from his notes. "We did the most due diligence on Alejandra Batista we could. Personal interviews with people outside her family and friends—former teachers, classmates, parish priest, even a Girl Scout leader. We told them the purpose of the interview was for a potential job position. I didn't think that would be a question that would skew the answers. Suffice to say, Allie had the highest standards of integrity, leadership, and interpersonal skills of anyone that the interviewees had known. We can keep digging, Tommy, but . . . she's totally clean."

"How many did you interview?" Tommy asked.

"Thirty-two," Tim answered.

"Keep asking around. I don't want any surprises. What about your hacker nerds? Any surprises there? Some Tinder date waiting to come out of the woodwork?"

Still reading from his notes, Tim said, "No online presence at all, really. No Facebook, no Twitter. No references to her on those or any other web sites. Everybody has something on the Web—not this girl. Her Social Security number checks, her addresses check, birth date, and parents—everything checks. There's just nothing associated with it of any interest."

"Keep looking. Imagine you've got the same resources as the Catholic Church is using to discredit her."

"Got it, Tommy. We'll do our best."

"All right, Silk, what do you have?'

Willis answered, "First, if we file this action, it will be a case of first impression. Our research shows that at no time, nowhere, has this cause of action been raised in any state or federal court. A state court would've been a reach because of the federal questions involved, but we checked anyway. Does a US District Court have jurisdiction over the Catholic Church? The answer is *yes*. The church has been sued several times in the sex-scandal cases, just not on ecclesiastical rules. But we have jurisdiction."

"So where does that leave us on the legal rights of the parties?" Tommy asked.

Willis continued, "We've got the Civil Rights Act of 1964 and its subsequent amendments prohibiting the discrimination of women for employment without just cause."

"What about the employee exclusion?" Tommy asked.

"We don't think it applies in this instance," Willis replied. "Our research indicates that a priest does not fit within the legal definition of an employee. At best, a priest would be considered an independent contractor."

Willis took a sip of his coffee before continuing. "Besides, we're seeking an injunction to prohibit the archdiocese from excluding Ms. Batista from the *seminary*. A seminarian does not receive income in any way, shape, or form, so therefore cannot be considered an employee. The seminarian is a student. It's *only after* ordination that a priest could arguably be an employee by taking a position within a diocese or order. If Ms. Batista were to win the lawsuit, go to the seminary, and become ordained, we could take that fight up at that time. She could also set up her own parish without the support of a diocese or order and not be employed by anyone.

"We also have case law expanding the rights of women beyond areas of employment, such as admission to venues that had been previously restricted to males. Venues like educational institutions, which a seminary certainly is. Shannon Faulkner vs. The Citadel, for example. Or US vs. VMI. But never a seminary.

"On the flip side, they've got the First Amendment right to the separation of church and state, which prevents federal law from interfering with the operations of any church."

"When I came in," Tommy said, "there seemed to be a debate going on. Enlighten me."

Willis again replied, "There's a difference of opinion about whether we can get past a motion for summary judgment. Of course, they'll argue that as a matter of law, the court has no jurisdiction over the issue and will dismiss the lawsuit. Plenty of gray area there. But it will all depend on the judge we draw."

Tommy took a sip of his coffee, looked at Tim Prentice, and asked, "Do you know who the most important person in the United States is?"

Tim had gotten this incorrect before and swore never again. "Federal district court judge."

"Exactly," Tommy answered. "A federal district court judge is appointed for life. The president must appease the voters and Congress to get anything done. Congress must appease the voters and the president to get anything done. The only oversights to a federal district court judge are the judges in the federal court of appeals, who are also federal judges appointed for life. Danielle, you do a lot of appellate work. Please explain to us the likelihood of overturning a federal district court judge on appeal."

Danielle leaned back in her chair. "The percentage of cases that are overruled by the appellate court is less than ten percent. The only appeal after that court's decision is to the US Supreme Court, which has the prerogative to decide whether to even *hear* the appeal or not. And the number of times they decide to hear an appeal is minuscule. Maybe less than a hundred a year, out of tens of thousands submitted."

Silk chimed in, "The United States federal court judge is king."

"That might be a little simplified, but he or she can have a greater direct effect on the law in one year by himself—or herself—than a single congressman can in a lifetime."

Tommy stroked his chin. "Willis, you said whether we get thrown out or not will depend upon the judge we draw?"

"Federal judges fall into two categories: conservative or progressive. Conservative judges tend to be strict constructionists who feel that the enactment of laws is the role of the legislature, and their role is to interpret that law. Progressive judges believe that the law is a growing body that has to be viewed with regard to an ever-changing society."

"So we need a progressive, I assume?" Tommy responded.

"It's basically a coin flip," Danielle interjected.

Tommy thought, Joe Bob would take fifty-fifty any time.

"Okay, Tommy, let's assume we can get to the jury. What's our story?" Willis asked.

"Pretty straight forward. The Catholic Church discriminates against women by barring them from the priesthood solely based on their gender," Tommy answered. "Now, this discrimination is legal, provided they have good reason to do so which is on the Church to prove."

Tommy got up, grabbed another beignet and paced alongside the table. "There is no biblical reference for denying women the priesthood. Jewish women in the time of Jesus were treated little better than slaves. One could argue behavior like that was normal at the time, and He might not have selected a woman apostle because of social norms. The church will counter that Jesus had treated women equally, much more so than anyone would or could expect at the time. So, given His even treatment of women—the Church will argue—a failure to choose female apostles was indeed intentional. The fact that many pagan religions at the time had priestesses would also support that argument."

"Makes sense to me. Who wants to watch a bunch of men dance around at Stonehenge?" Silk asked.

Tommy responded, "I don't think it makes sense at all. We know about these other religions in hindsight. Jesus lived in a very specific time and place. He was fulfilling the Jewish scriptures and was working within the Hebrew faith. That faith had no priestesses at the time, so the fact that pagan religions did so was irrelevant. Why would Jews have cared about what pagans did? His limiting the gender of the apostles to men would have been a practical solution to promote acceptance of His teachings by His mostly Jewish followers. I think the real story lies with what happened *after* Jesus."

Tommy took a bite of pastry and pressed on with his argument. "Since all the apostles were Jewish males in a society where the status of a female was just above a slave, it's not surprising that none of the early Christian men felt compelled to ordain a woman. Women were inferior beings and therefore could not be in a leadership role. The same treatment of women by the Catholic Church has unfortunately continued beyond early Christian times. I remember when I was a boy, women had to have their heads covered before entering the Church. They couldn't enter the sanctuary except for cleaning purposes. They couldn't read scripture from the pulpit. They couldn't act as Mass servers, and they couldn't touch sacred items such as the chalice. They couldn't sing in the Church choir, and they couldn't distribute communion. Today they can do all those things. Yet they still can't be priests."

Tommy's passion flared up. "If the situation regarding women was like that just *fifty* years ago, just think what it must have been like *two thousand* years ago."

Tommy took a sip of coffee and continued, "So the fact is simply this: Christ did not name a female apostle. That's it. The Catholic Church's story is that the omission was on purpose, to exclude women forever from the priesthood. If the jury believes that, then the Church has a good reason to do what they do. My story is that there were many other reasons why He did not name a woman as an apostle—any one of which could explain His actions, and any one of which could tilt the scales of justice in our favor. I like our odds. Their burden will be to prove their position in one way only, and we have the option to prove our position with one of many.

"I think the Church is really stretching to come up with the 'he didn't do something on purpose' argument to justify two thousand years of sexual discrimination. Since they have no direct, divine revelation from the scriptures, they're relying on divine revelation by omission. It's a pretty thin slice."

Randi interjected. "Surely that's not the extent of their case?"

"They'll have other arguments, but they're all used to support the basic premise that because Jesus didn't do something, He meant that it should last forever. Then there's the fact that Pope John Paul II, whom Catholics believe was infallible, explicitly banned the practice in 1994," Tommy answered. "Pope Francis backed him up recently; he basically said the ban will continue forever."

"Catholics believe that a man is infallible?" Randi asked.

"Many do," Tommy replied. "Lucky for us, all we have to care about is what the people in that jury box believe."

Danielle responded, "If the jury believes our story, six or twelve people could make a lot of Catholics hopping mad."

"Can't make an omelet without breaking a billion eggs," Tommy said hopefully.

Randi countered, "I'm not sure that analogy works here."

"Well, come up with a better one. We'll need it for the press," Tommy responded. The table finally felt comfortable enough to laugh.

Tommy paused and asked, "So let's get started." Tommy

rose and the rest followed suit and everyone began to gather their notes.

"Danielle and Randi, draft the complaint. The defendants are the Archdiocese of New Orleans and Archbishop Sierra. Silk, review their draft and throw it over to me this afternoon. I want to file it tomorrow morning if we can. Tim, get me a list of Catholic theologians and scholars, hopefully ordained, who have come out in opposition to the Church's position on this issue. I suspect there may be more than a few. Interview those that you can. See if any will testify."

Tommy continued as they all filed out into the outer office. "Also, there are psychologists and psychiatrists who do interviews with potential applicants to the seminary. Find out who they are in this archdiocese and ask them if they would be willing to interview Allie, as if they were interviewing a male applicant, and judge her accordingly. If we can get by the gender disqualification, I don't want her being denied admittance on a technicality later."

Tim looked up from taking his notes and nodded. "Anybody got anything else?" Tommy asked.

Willis suddenly piped up, "Wait."

Everyone stopped and turned back to him.

"Yes, Silk?" Tommy asked.

"Maybe I'm stating the obvious here, but I just want to be clear."

"Okay?"

They all waited.

"I didn't get into this business to pick low-hanging fruit. We're taking the case. We're going to battle one of the most powerful organizations in the world in court."

The moment hung in the air and everyone traded glances until Tommy broke the silence.

"Anybody want out?" he asked.

A chorus of "We're in!" and "Let's do it!" filled the lobby. Then Betty chimed in, "So get to work already!"

CHAPTER FIFTEEN

"Allie, this is Tommy Riley. How are you?"

"I'm very curious today, Mr. Riley. How are you?"

Tommy laughed. He loved Allie's dry sense of humor. "Allie, if you have any reservations at all, now is the time to speak up. Because once we file the complaint, we're going down this road and there's no turning back. You understand that, right?"

"You're filing the complaint?" she asked.

"Tomorrow morning," he replied.

"Which would imply that you're taking my case," she pointed out and waited for his response.

Staring out his office window, Tommy finally answered, "We're in this together now, Allie."

"Thank you, Mr. Riley. I prayed to God about this. God has led *you* to *me*."

Tommy laughed, "I would quibble with that because it's what I do. God has led you to me."

It was Allie's turn to laugh, "Incorrect. You think I picked your name out the Yellow Pages, Mr. Riley? You must believe me when I tell you that God led *you* to *me*."

Her unyielding sincerity momentarily made Tommy slightly uncomfortable, so he reminded himself that this quality would prove invaluable at trial. He returned to the matter at hand. "Certainly a welcome referral then, from the man upstairs. But I asked you about your doubt in taking this on?"

"Oh, yes, of course. My answer to your question is a resounding no. I don't have the slightest doubt. This is not only the right thing to do, it is also what must be done."

"No one has brought a case like this against the Catholic Church before. They will use any tool in their immense arsenal to uncover or fabricate anything they can use against us. And that's not all you have to worry about. The media will be all over this. Like it or not, you're about to become a celebrity. You need to prepare yourself for the fight of your life."

"I'm a Latina American woman living in the Deep South," Allie answered dryly. "I've been fighting my entire life."

Tommy smiled broadly. "They have no idea what they're up against. We'll talk very soon. Goodbye, Allie."

†

On Tuesday morning, a complaint was filed electronically in the United States Federal Court, Eastern District of Louisiana, alleging that the Archdiocese of New Orleans and the Archbishop of the Diocese, Archbishop Jorge Sierra, were in violation of the Civil Rights Act of 1964 in denying Alejandra Batista acceptance to the St. Joseph seminary in Covington, Louisiana. Upon receipt by the District Court, the action was placed into the computer for a random and immediate draw of the judge to whom the case would be assigned. The name drawn was United States Federal District Court Judge John Bateman. A summons was issued electronically back to the offices of the Riley Law Group. Upon receipt, Betty Lincoln made a copy and gave it to the process server the firm normally used. By two o'clock that afternoon, the process was duly served upon His Eminence, Archbishop Jorge Sierra and the archdiocese. The wheels of justice were now in motion.

†

By 4:00 p.m. Eastern standard time, Monsignor Enrico "Rick" Renzulli had called his adjunct into his office, located in the heart of Washington D.C. In his hand was a copy of the complaint from the office of the archdiocese. Renzulli was the general counsel of the United States Conference of Catholic Bishops, and he was about to become a very big thorn in Tommy Riley's side.

When his loyal adjunct entered the office, Renzulli got right to the point.

"Father Murray, I've just sent you a copy of a complaint filed today in New Orleans federal court. I want you to read it and begin an immediate investigation into Alejandra Batista, of New Orleans, Louisiana, and her attorney, Thomas Patrick Riley. Also notify the Chairman of the Conference of Catholic Bishops and send him a copy of the lawsuit, with a copy to the Solicitor General at the Vatican."

"Right away, Monsignor," said Father Murray as he left the office.

Monsignor Renzulli leaned back in his chair and stared out at the Capitol. A brilliant lawyer, he had grown weary of the predictable sex-abuse cases, along with their inevitable outcomes. As a committed priest, he had also tired of their seediness, of the way they went beyond mere jurisprudence and cut to the core of Christian beliefs. This was something new. It piqued his interest. It had an element of surprise, and to his knowledge had never been filed before.

He wondered where this Southern lawyer had trained. Probably Tulane, he smirked. A New Orleans attorney wouldn't present much of a challenge for the mind of Rick Renzulli. The First Amendment was very clear about the separation of church and state. He could undoubtedly get the case dismissed on a motion for summary judgment. His mood soured as he thought of New Orleans itself, the stifling climate, and the gaudy revelers wallowing in sin.

He should be prepared to spend some time in the archbishop's residence in New Orleans. A born social climber, he would finally get the chance to get to know Archbishop Sierra better. Sierra was a young man for the position, and his rise had been swift. It never hurt to have more friends in high places. If nothing else, the overwhelming totality of his victory would impress the archbishop, and those to whom he reported.

CHAPTER SIXTEEN

Renzulli had worked in his parents' law office during the summer while in the high-school seminary, and had continued there during the summers while in the collegiate seminary. His love of the law was matched only by his love for the Church; the combination of the two seemed a natural fit. After graduation and ordination, he requested that the vocation office allow him to attend law school. Based upon his outstanding academic record and attitude, the diocese granted his request. He took the LSAT, and his near-perfect score ensured acceptance to Harvard Law School where he graduated in the top ten percent of his class. After graduation, he was accepted to study for a doctorate in canon law at the Holy See in Rome. After obtaining his Ph.D., he stayed in Rome and worked in the Vatican on legal affairs affecting the Catholic Church. In addition to English, he also became fluent in Italian and Latin.

Years later when the priest-related sex scandals broke in the United States, Renzulli was sent back to work with the United States Conference of Catholic Bishops. While he initially had directed local counsel in the Church's defense, he soon began to participate in the trials themselves and became an adept litigator. Despite frequent losses in court, Renzulli and his superiors took solace in knowing that without him outcomes could have been much worse.

Now in his mid-40s, he was recognized and highly regarded in both church canon-law circles and civil-law circles. Along with good genes, the years had been kind to him and age seemed to enhance his forceful appearance. When he occasionally appeared in public without his Roman collar, people often mistook him for a French actor or a Formula One race-car driver. Rick Renzulli was at the top of his game.

He walked into his office that morning with a decision. Once again, he called Father Murray into his office.

"Father, I want to file an answer in the Alejandra Batista litigation Friday morning. I also want to file a motion for summary judgment and request an immediate hearing on the motion. I want to get this dismissed as soon as we can before the media even gets wind of it. It'll be bad enough as it is. The basis of the motion will be the Church's rights under the First Amendment, of course, accompanied by a legal brief containing appropriate case and statutory law supporting the motion. I think it's important to strike quickly so that Thomas Patrick Riley, Esquire, knows his opposition is well prepared for litigation. It'll send the same message to the judge assigned to the case. The Catholic Church will not be railroaded into changing a doctrine that has stood for two thousand years."

"Of course, Monsignor. We'll select local counsel today, send them our answer, motion, and brief by Thursday afternoon to be filed Friday. We'll have local counsel move to have you admitted to practice law in the Eastern District of Louisiana as well." Father Murray shifted into a more conversational tone.

"If I may say so, Monsignor, it'll be nice to have a case we can finally win."

Monsignor Renzulli stared at his assistant, but said nothing. He was thinking the exact same thing.

CHAPTER SEVENTEEN

As Tommy walked into the office Betty greeted him with a cup of chicory coffee and a concerned look. "Morning, boss. Looks like you jumped into a snake pit, and these snakes are wearing crosses."

Tommy had been expecting something he just wasn't sure what. "Let me have it."

"They filed their answer this morning. Nothing surprising, I e-mailed it to you. Moved for summary judgment, with an accompanying brief of thirty-five pages. It's all in the e-mail, but they essentially call you a liar."

Tommy couldn't help but chuckle as they entered his office. "Now that doesn't sound very Christian."

"Also says you don't know squat, because you have no business filing this lawsuit in federal court and the judge should throw it out," Betty said crisply. "I could have told them you don't know squat."

Tommy moved toward his desk. "Can I get a paper copy please? I hate reading briefs on the computer."

"It's on your desk," she said as she left.

A half hour later, he'd finished reading. He was impressed by the brief, and more than a little irritated by the impressive résumé of the monsignor attached to the case. He picked up the phone and called in Gerald Grant.

Gerald was a brilliant lawyer. However, he had a setback that prevented him from becoming a top litigator: he was deaf. He read lips unfailingly and spoke eloquently, but many firms wouldn't risk putting Gerald in front of a judge, jury—or even a client. A trial lawyer had to react quickly and assuredly to any words spoken, whether he was facing the speaker or not. Tommy, in a stroke of genius, realized that having a master lip-reader on his staff would prove invaluable in court. By now every lawyer in New Orleans knew to cover their mouth with papers when they spoke to co-counsel, like an NFL coach. But Gerald was invaluable to him in other ways—he was also a clever and erudite contributor to the Riley Law Group research and legal briefs.

"What's up, Tommy?" Gerald asked as he walked into his office.

"So . . . we're suing the Catholic Church," Tommy replied.

"I think I overheard something to that effect," Gerald said, smiling.

Tommy smiled back. "Take a look at their answer and brief in support of the motion for summary judgement. Randi and Danielle have researched our legal standing to bring the suit in federal court. Talk with them so you can prepare our response."

"How quickly do you want this?" Gerald asked.

"As soon as you can deliver it. I want them to know that if they want to fast track this, we're ready to go. Also, on your way out, ask Betty to notify Judge Bateman's office that we have no objection to the motion to admit this Monsignor Renzulli. He'll grant it anyway, but there isn't a judge in this state who doesn't enjoy being deferred to."

As Gerald got up to leave, Tommy motioned for him to wait for one more directive.

"Oh! And Gerald, their brief is thirty-five pages. Make ours thirty-six," he said, smiling.

†

Every Friday afternoon, Rebecca Gomez, a court clerk in the US district federal court, would take an hour after work and review the cases that had been filed during the week. She had an agreement with Bruce Wilkes, a reporter for *The Times-Picayune*. In exchange for fifty dollars, she would send him any noteworthy cases filed during the week that he could use for the "City and State" section of the paper. After she had read the complaint and answer in the Batista litigation, she picked up the phone and called Wilkes; she was put through immediately.

"I need one hundred for this one, Bruce," she said.

Wilkes sighed. He had no compunction about paying for good info, but if you couldn't keep a lid on bribe inflation the whole system was out of hand. "You know the rate, Rebecca."

"Fine. I've got a dozen bloggers I can e-mail it to by pushing a button." He heard the phone click. He felt a burning ball of acid start to well up in his chest. There had been rumors that the newspaper he worked for, which had served New Orleans since 1837, was considering ceasing publication of their print edition. He dialed the number. "Okay, Rebecca. You know what? I'm feeling generous today."

As she began to speak, the ball of acid in his chest slowly evaporated. After she had summarized the complaint and answer, Bruce said, "E-mail me what you've got. If it is what you say it is, I'll give you two hundred."

Once Bruce Wilkes read Rebecca's e-mail, he could barely type his story fast enough. He thought it was a good story; it had human interest and might even end up on the front page of the local section. He had the jump and was grateful for that; he knew the TV cameras would likely push him out of the way once it broke. Of course, he had contacted this Alejandra Batista and she had declined to comment, but he felt like he knew what she was about already. Wilkes had been Catholic since day one. What kind of a woman wanted to become a priest? Gender identity stories had become reliable click-bait, and he could see it now: "Local Sister Wants to Become a Father." *The Church will never put up with this*, he thought.

His editor, Mike Alford, saw things from a different perspective. Raised Protestant but agnostic for years, Alford had been a cub reporter in Boston when the priest sex-abuse scandal broke there. He remembered vividly the way it scandalized the community and titillated readers. He knew this story was big.

When Saturday's morning edition arrived on his doorstep, Bruce Wilkes was shocked to see his name above the fold on the front page of the main section. The headline read: "More Headaches Ahead for Catholic Church: Local Nun Sues Over Gender Discrimination." Excited and a little scared, he opened his web browser to the newspaper's homepage. His story had already generated over 100 comments and it had only been online for an hour.

CHAPTER EIGHTEEN

That same Friday, while Rebecca was striking headline gold for Bruce Wilkes, Judge John Bateman met with his staff attorneys to go over cases filed during the week to which he had been assigned. First up were the criminal cases that invariably clogged his docket because of the immediate attention they required. Next was the civil docket.

Just when Judge Bateman was seeing visions of happy-hour oysters at restaurant Lüke dancing in his head, Dick Cole, his lead staff attorney, piped up. "I saved the best for last. Plaintiff Alejandra Batista has filed suit against the Catholic Church under the Civil Rights Act of 1964, requesting a mandatory injunction to allow her into the seminary. And get this: she wants a jury trial, leaving the question of equitable relief up to you."

Cole continued, "The defendants are the Archdiocese of New Orleans and Archbishop Jorge Sierra. Today we received a general denial of all claims, and obviously they want dismissal by summary judgment. Neither party has requested any discovery."

"No discovery? That's unusual," Judge Bateman said. John Bateman had a reputation for moving his docket along like a

Ford Motor plant. His pet peeve was a plaintiff's attorney who filed a lawsuit and then spent the next two years issuing legal interrogatories and taking depositions. Woe to the attorney who went on a fishing expedition in his courtroom.

"Who is the plaintiff's attorney?" Judge Bateman asked.

"Tommy Riley," Cole responded.

"Oh, boy, sure sounds like him," Judge Bateman said. "And on the other side?"

Dick Cole responded, reading from his notes. "The New Orleans based firm Colby and Colby is acting as local counsel for Monsignor Enrico Renzulli, general counsel for the United States Conference of Catholic Bishops. They attached his CV—Harvard law, Ph.D. in canon law from the Vatican. It goes on."

Bateman knew the drill. "I'm sure it does. Well, let me just get down on my poor, uneducated Southern knees and genuflect to my East Coast superiors."

Cole responded, "They have requested an expedited hearing for summary judgment. Naturally, Colby and Colby have moved to have him admitted to the Eastern District of Louisiana for the sole purpose of this litigation. Riley has no objection."

"Of course, he doesn't—the kiss-ass. I'll sign off, like I've got a choice. In the meantime, we'll wait for Mr. Riley's response to the motion. Knowing Riley, he'll want to move this along; he's one of the quickest lawyers in town. Amazing how that works when you don't bill by the hour. The media will come sniffing, if they're not already. Remind everyone there will be no cameras in the courtroom. I'll probably issue a contempt citation or two, just at random. Keep 'em on their toes. Expedited hearing. This Renzulli sure sounds like a piece of work, and probably a colossal pain in our collective derriere."

With that, Judge Bateman rose from the table. "If that's all there is, I've got a corner booth waiting for me," Judge Bateman said cordially.

†

John Bateman had been appointed to the federal bench by President Clinton after a distinguished career as a litigator for a major New Orleans law firm. He had been active in the Democratic Party since college, and despite some minor opposition from a handful of Republican senators, he had been readily approved by the senate since both Republican senators from Louisiana had supported his appointment. During his years on the bench, he had developed a reputation as a progressive judge.

As he drove down Saint Charles Avenue toward Luke, he considered the Batista case. Bateman loved all his cases, because he loved just about everything in his life. But this one had a chance to be even more interesting than most. He was relieved he had not been born Catholic, not that he had anything against it. But if he had been a Catholic, he might have had to recuse himself and miss this possibly very fascinating case. Judge John Bateman did not think about organized religion much at all. His "religion" was anything that moved him. And right now, the only thing he felt religious about was the Tabasco sauce hovering over his beloved oysters, and the bottle of Rombauer chardonnay that awaited him in a silver ice bucket, starting to sweat.

CHAPTER NINETEEN

When Bruce Wilkes' article in *The Times-Picayune* published, it was picked up and read, e-mailed, and Tweeted—from Marigny to Metairie. It also landed at the door of one true believer, who was not known to most of the other Catholics in New Orleans.

Saturday morning, this man read Bruce Wilkes's article in *The Times-Picayune* no less than six times; with each read, he grew more incensed. He knew better than anyone what it took to be a priest. The mere notion of a woman being ordained as a fully functioning priest nearly brought his breakfast back up. This was heresy, a crime against the Church. In the old days, it would have been dealt with summarily by torture, and if necessary, by death. Compromise was not a component of the Church that Michel knew. Holy Mother Church had become soft with her political correctness. He longed for the old days when the Church was as feared as it was respected. He took a deep breath and tried to calm himself. He knew Monsignor Renzulli's reputation was that of an excellent priest and an excellent lawyer. With God's help, he would be able to prevent this travesty from happening. Michel also knew he'd have a front-row seat to the proceedings. He would watch over the lawsuit carefully as it proceeded; if it started going badly, he was prepared to do whatever had to be done. God would guide him.

He glared at his cell phone, lying inert next to his wallet and keys. They must have read the news by now. This was news that would travel at the speed of light to Rome, to the priory in Switzerland, to his minders in Paris. It would be getting late there, but surely they had taken the time to meet?

His cell phone buzzed harshly, as if responding to his thoughts. He just stared at it, at the +33 prefix number to which he had pledged every aspect of his life. Finally he reached for it. "Oui, c'est Michel." His French was still excellent, but it had been a while since he had studied, and he wasn't ready for the overwhelming speed of the invective that poured out of the tiny device. The meaning, however, was easy to grasp. It must stop. *It must stop now.* "D'accord," he responded, "d'accord." The French plea for "Got it. I understand, now let me go." Finally the device ceased its eruptions.

With that, he stood up, smoothed the wrinkles in his cassock, and went to Mass.

CHAPTER TWENTY

By Monday morning, news of the lawsuit had gone nuclear. Every news organization on earth had reported the story, including the refusal of the Archdiocese of New Orleans to comment on any ongoing litigation. Calls to the Riley Law Group went unanswered, and some sources noted it was unusual for a plaintiff's attorney not to seek publicity for himself or herself, the client, and the case. And it was no surprise that each of various national-news outlets held tightly to their points of view.

The *Wall Street Journal's* front-page headline read "God's Law versus Federal Law." The reporter had interviewed theologians and Catholic scholars about the basis of the Church's view on the matter. She had interviewed practicing attorneys and constitutional-law professors. The article concluded that the case was groundbreaking litigation and would probably be resolved at the appellate level, regardless of how things went in trial court.

The New York Times also ran a front-page article. While dutifully reporting the opinions of those interviewed, the paper noted that the Church was resistant to change, and the paper felt the rights of the individual should outweigh the antiquated practices of the Church.

Fox News took a more conservative approach and devoted fifteen minutes in its morning segment on the litigation. At midday, two different practicing attorneys debated the issue. Monday evening, the news anchor ended her program with a discussion of the case and concluded that the constitutional guarantee of the freedom of religion prevented the Catholic Church from any interference by the state in the Church's ecclesiastical rules.

Not surprisingly, MSNBC took the opposing view. They opined that no individual person or individual institution was above the law; as such, the Catholic Church could not operate outside the law. Discrimination of women was illegal in the United States, and the Church could either abide by the law or get out.

The one thing each news organization had in common was the desire to uncover Alejandra Batista and broadcast her story to the world. Each of them failed. Requests for interviews went unanswered and they eventually gave up.

†

When Tommy reached his office that morning, six news trucks with the requisite rooftop satellite dishes were there to greet him. Reporters, microphones, and film crews rushed him. Tommy managed to move through the chaos to slip inside, relatively unharmed. In here, it was always business as usual and he could finally exhale. Betty was waiting, like any other day.

Betty got right to business. "*60 Minutes* has called three times. That's a first. I'd give anything to see you on TV."

"No interviews," Tommy answered quickly.

"You sure? It might get Leroy and Benjamin to watch something other than *Dancing with the Stars*."

"Who am I to ruin their prime time viewing?" Tommy said as he started toward his office.

Moving back to her desk, Betty called out, "We have definitely arrived, because we even got a death threat." She adopted a low, villainous voice. "'God promises immediate death to the heretics and all who support this profanity!'"

"Better get used to it." Just before he reached his office, he stopped. "Just to be safe, call Sergeant Yardley. Ask him if he can throw us a couple off-duty cops on rotations. Tell him we'll double their rate. Suggest that he remind the jackals out there this is private property. Also, call Allie and see if the news media has discovered where she lives. If they haven't found her, tell her to find a place to lie low."

Inside the relative quiet of his office, Tommy checked his computer and saw an e-mail from Gerald Grant with a rough draft of the response brief to the Church's motion for summary judgment.

By the end of the afternoon, the team was comfortable with their response and its supporting law. It was one-half page longer than the defendants' brief. Tommy had to laugh. He gave the okay to file their response the next morning, with a request for an expedited hearing on the defendants' motion. They were as anxious to get it heard as Renzulli was.

When Tommy left that evening, he noticed the NOPD officers had removed the news media from the property. Three news trucks followed him home, but the security at New Orleans Towers shooed them off. Penthouse living certainly had its privileges. *That's something Joe Bob would have said,* Tommy thought.

CHAPTER TWENTY-ONE

Michel was infuriated. He flipped through the news channels, in desperate search of a sign the world hadn't tilted off its axis. The Godless media seemed intent on turning the heretic's case against the Church into a reality soap opera, ignoring the very real and potentially catastrophic damage that could result. A fundamental principle of the Faith, laid down by the Lord Jesus Christ Himself, was being undermined. How ridiculous to even consider that a man-made law of the government, any government, could overrule the will of God. Certainly, Satan was at work through this Batista woman. There could be no doubt.

But he took a breath, steadied himself, and leaned on his faith in the Lord. So far, the case had amounted to little more than noise. The archdiocese had filed for a motion to dismiss. Certainly that motion would be granted and all of this would be over and forgotten. He would be there to watch over the proceedings himself, and would pray on the matter ceaselessly until the hearing. Should the unthinkable occur, he would not sit idly by as the case made its way through trial.

The elders in France had made themselves very clear. This must stop, it had to stop—and surely they intended for him to stop it. He would be prepared to stop this heretic and her heretic lawyer himself. Threatening phone calls would no longer suffice. He began to develop a more effective plan.

CHAPTER TWENTY-TWO

Tuesday morning, in the guest quarters of Archbishop Sierra's residence, Monsignor Renzulli was enjoying a cappuccino while reading the Riley Law Group's response to his motion for summary judgment. He was impressed by the legal argument, and more than a little surprised. He knew there were great legal minds in this part of the South, he just didn't understand why any of them would work for Tommy Riley. He had expected a rudimentary response; certainly nothing as polished or as eloquent as the document he had before him. Surely this prose was beyond Riley's talents. But whoever had written the brief had done an excellent job of presenting the plaintiff's position. While Monsignor Renzulli was confident in his motion, their response was just as strong. He knew instinctively that the result could go either way, depending on the judge. He had to be prepared to try the case.

He read in detail the investigation reports on Riley and Alejandra Batista. He had to admit, Batista would be an excellent candidate for the priesthood if her name had been Alejandro. She seemed an exceptional woman.

Riley was a different matter. There didn't seem to be anything exceptional about the man at all; it just seemed he was always in the right place at the right time. He was a lucky man and luck eventually runs out. His high success rate in the cases he tried did not correspond with his mediocre academic record. Renzulli supposed that the University of Texas was a slight improvement over Tulane, but not by much. He assumed he wasn't dazzling juries and judges with his brilliance, so it had to be something else. He needed to meet Riley and take the measure of the man. The rules of the Eastern District required counsel for both parties to have a meeting prior to trial to discuss any potential settlement. The rules did not specify a time frame in which the meeting should occur. Monsignor Renzulli thought there was no time like the present.

CHAPTER TWENTY-THREE

"Step into my parlor, said the spider to the fly," Betty chirped to Tommy on Wednesday morning. "The monsignor has requested a meeting at his office."

"Not wasting any time is he. When?" Tommy asked.

"He said up to you, but any time Friday. Preferably in the morning; 10 a.m., if that's convenient," Betty replied.

"Up to me. Can't wait," Tommy said. "Did he say anything else?"

"I spoke to his assistant, Father Michael Murray. He sounded like an eager student who had just finished his homework and had no life. He said it was in conformance with court rules requiring settlement discussions."

"That's strange. Surely he's not seeking a settlement. There's no middle ground. Allie's either admitted to the seminary or she isn't."

Betty rolled her eyes. "There's always a middle ground. You know that. Our client might become a very wealthy—though ecclesiastically frustrated—young woman."

Tommy shook his head. "I wish. It would save us a lot of grief. But I don't think so, Betty; not this one."

Betty laughed, "I know, I know, Saint Batista. This one's different."

As Tommy headed towards his office, he grumbled, "It's like I'm being called in to the headmaster's office."

"Where I went to school, we called him the Principal," Betty joked. "But either way, you might be in for a good paddling."

Tommy reviewed the transcripts of the interviews conducted by Tim Prentice and his team. Most of the interviews were with Catholic Church scholars and theologians who did not support the Church's position on a male-only priesthood. He had completed several, and Prentice had indicated he had limited the initial group geographically to Louisiana and the South. The priests who had been interviewed had been excommunicated because of their position on this issue. Tommy worried that defrocked priests might not be the best witnesses to put in front of a jury, and that he might open himself up to ambushes from the other side.

On one hand, these former priests had made a tremendous sacrifice to speak up for what they believed to be true. If he could paint their excommunication from the priesthood as the ultimate display of their beliefs and their faith, the jury might sympathize. On the other hand, Monsignor Renzulli would be able to impeach their testimony as the rantings of a rogue group. He would undoubtedly point out that of the thousands of priests in the United States, only a few had adopted this position contrary to the Vatican. Two priests that Prentice's team had uncovered were covertly championing a change in the gender issue and would not testify. They were also out of the jurisdiction of the Eastern District's subpoena power, so Tommy could not force them to do so. But he would not do that in any event, since he was reluctant to put on hostile witnesses to support his case.

The scholars and theologians who weren't priests were another matter. They were very vocal about the lack of divine revelation to support the Church's stand and had written articles and books on the issue. They were more than willing to testify. Tommy knew, however, that for each witness Tommy put on, Renzulli would be able to put on two or more to counter his witnesses. A trial of competing experts could take weeks or even months to finish, depending on how many witnesses each side wished to call. Tommy always tried to avoid jury fatigue, especially in this case when he was challenging a well-established status quo.

Tommy also knew that Judge Bateman would not be happy about, or even agree to, a trial that long. Then he had an idea. An idea that would almost certainly shorten the trial to a day or two and might accelerate a trial setting. It would be brazen, but it could work.

CHAPTER TWENTY-FOUR

Manuel pulled the black Lincoln Town Car up to the offices of the archdiocese at five minutes until ten on Friday morning. As usual, Manuel said very little. Tommy had remembered Paddy telling him, "Manny is blank as a check, but he can drive like a pro. He's also smart enough not to talk about what he hears." After dropping Tommy off, he'd find a coffee shop nearby and wait for the call to pick up his boss. This suited him fine since Manny enjoyed the calm environs of coffee-house culture, a fact that may have come as a surprise to Tommy; he would never have suspected Manny was interested in much beyond the sports-talk radio that accompanied their drives together.

†

The archdiocese was headquartered in a three-story white building and, with the adjacent cathedral, took up a whole city block near the French Quarter.

Tommy walked into the prestigious and professionally appointed lobby. He walked up to a young priest seated at a gigantic, dark wooden desk.

"Mr. Riley," the priest stated coldly. Before Tommy could answer, the priest continued in his even tone, "Sit down and I will tell the monsignor you are here."

I'm famous, Tommy thought, before walking over to one of the lounge chairs in the waiting area. He heard the priest say into the phone, "Please tell Monsignor Renzulli that *he* is here," and had to laugh to himself, thinking, *he makes me sound like Darth Vader*.

Tommy took note of the surroundings. On one wall was the most magnificent crucifix he had ever seen, almost threatening. A weapon? He acknowledged he was just projecting, given the situation. On the other wall hung a picture of Pope Francis beside a picture of Archbishop Sierra.

The coffee table in front of him had numerous Catholic publications and news periodicals. The current issue of *Time* magazine caught his attention. The cover had a cross that was burning with the caption, "Is the Catholic Church being forced into a new age?"

As Tommy reached for the magazine, another priest entered the lobby and curtly instructed him to follow. Trailing behind the stoic figure in black, Tommy could no longer suppress the wisecracks the grim environment had inspired since he arrived.

"Question. You guys still go in for corporal punishment? Paddles, rulers, that kind of thing? My secretary wants to know," he asked.

The man, of course, offered no reply as he ushered Tommy into an empty office furnished with four low, plush leather chairs similar to the couch in the lobby. They circled a bare coffee table that featured some of the most ornate woodworking Tommy had ever seen. In the corner, another gigantic wooden power desk completed the Wall Street meets Vatican décor.

As his chaperone closed the door to leave, Tommy decided to get in one more barb.

"Yes, coffee would be great, Alfred. Cream and sugar."

The door slammed shut. Tommy chuckled to himself again. "Or not. That's fine, too."

A few minutes later, a slim man in his forties walked in. He wore a priest's cassock; but instead of the white Roman collar, he wore purple. He didn't require such accoutrements to appear more regal than he naturally was, but the collar certainly drove home the point: This was a man of consequence.

As for Monsignor Renzulli's initial impression of Tommy, the first thing he noticed were the pale-blue eyes framed by the tan complexion and the confident smile that accompanied a firm handshake. It was clear, to his disappointment, that the purple collar and the opulent surroundings did not intimidate Riley at all. *On the contrary,* Renzulli thought, *this man's countenance spoke to a genuine affection for a good fight.* Even a spiritual man could appreciate that kind of earthly confidence.

After brief introductions, the pair sat down opposite each other, the coffee table between them.

Tommy decided to get right to the point. "I appreciate the invitation, Monsignor. But since we both know a settlement in this case is impossible, I assume you called this meeting for other reasons?"

"Indeed, there can be no settlement, Mr. Riley. On that we can agree. Can I call you Tommy?"

"We were off to a good start, Monsignor. Let's keep it that way. You probably can't wait to get this up in front of a jury, am I right?"

Renzulli was not unaware of the man's arrogance, but decided to let it slide for the moment. "Aren't you getting ahead of yourself?" Monsignor Renzulli asked smugly. "If the judge rules in our favor on the summary judgment, there will be no facts to determine and no trial. The decision of the Church will remain as it is now. Now and forever, Tommy."

It was Tommy's turn to stew. They were roughly the same age, yet Renzulli was condescending in the manner of an older, superior man. "Now and forever. Who's getting ahead of themselves, Monsignor? First, I like our odds on summary judgment," Tommy replied firmly. "Second, only my friends call me Tommy. So I guess this conversation is over," he said as he started to stand up from his chair.

Renzulli realized he'd overstepped and raised his hand to calm Tommy. "Okay, counselor, okay. Please sit. I did not mean to offend you, and you are correct. We may or may not have a trial. Out of our hands for the moment," Monsignor Renzulli said pleasantly. "Please, may I offer you a coffee?" He rang a bell.

A minute later, a young priest served each of them a gigantic cappuccino, in a Wedgwood cup on an antique mother-of-pearl saucer. The massive cross drawn expertly in the foam had the effect Renzulli had hoped it might: Tommy laughed when he saw it.

"Bravo. Part of your influence here, or do you travel with your own barista?" Tommy motioned a toast in Renzulli's direction before he took a sip. "This is good. Very good."

Renzulli smiled broadly, teeth glinting. "I had the beans sent especially for you. Roasted in the Vatican itself. I'll send you the bag once the motion for summary judgment is accepted."

Tommy let the remark slide; he was enjoying the coffee way too much to argue.

"I guess I hoped someone with an Italian mother might appreciate a good cappuccino," Renzulli stated.

"You've done your homework," Tommy said, with grudging respect.

"As I'm sure you have." Renzulli continued, "Yes, I know a few things about you. Not much, but enough. I know you're Catholic."

"Come now, Monsignor," Tommy said smiling. "I'm sure your investigators uncovered a lot more about me than just that. Me, I suppose I'm more interested in the jury and witnesses."

Monsignor Renzulli took a sip of his cappuccino, set the saucer down, and said, "Then there's no disagreement that you are a Catholic. No conflict of interest?"

"Not really," Tommy said. "I believe in the core doctrine of the Catholic Church, the teachings of Jesus as revealed by the scriptures. To me that does not include the man-made rules of the cardinals or popes, which go way beyond what I consider the Word of God."

Renzulli stiffened slightly, and prodded mockingly, "What *you* consider the Word of God. I would be so interested to hear your thoughts on the matter."

Tommy took another sip of coffee. "I realize you have no interest in my opinion at all. But you brought me here to get inside my head. And these opinions cut to the core beliefs of the Church, if the case does make it to trial," Tommy answered.

"Please go on," Monsignor Renzulli replied, intrigued.

"God gave Moses and the Hebrews the Ten Commandments. The seventh commandment said, 'Thou shall not commit adultery.' Being the Lord, He could have said anything He wanted to say. He could have commanded, 'Thou shalt not engage in premarital sex,' or 'sex outside of marriage.' But He didn't. He said not to commit adultery, which is defined as a married person having sex with a person who is not his or her spouse. If God had said, 'Thou shalt not have sex outside of marriage,' then He would have covered premarital sex, extramarital sex, and adultery. But He didn't. He limited the ban to adultery. But the Church has expanded the commandment to prohibit any sex outside of marriage."

"Interesting interpretation," Monsignor Renzulli said. "The church believes it has been divinely revealed that the purpose of sex is to strengthen the bonds of marriage. Also, of course, to create families through procreation. That would limit sex to people who are married to one another.

"I certainly don't wish to condescend your level of religious study, whatever it may be," Renzulli purred, condescendingly. "But the law of Moses, the Old Testament, was superseded by the laws of our Lord and savior Jesus Christ in the New Testament. Bringing the Ten Commandments several millennia into the future has entailed a more thorough rendering than what can be inscribed with crude tools on a massive stone. I'm sure you understand."

"Oh, I understand," Tommy said, smiling, "But God didn't say that, did he? Man did."

"Are you familiar with the term 'cafeteria Catholic'?" Monsignor Renzulli asked.

"Sure," Tommy replied. "Someone who picks and chooses what teachings of the Church he wishes to accept."

"Precisely," Renzulli agreed. "As one picks and chooses food in a cafeteria. A true Catholic accepts all teachings of the Church. And if he cannot accept even one precept, he is not a true Catholic."

"It's a real catch-22," Tommy mocked. But the jibe knocked Renzulli off balance.

"Mr. Riley, your reliance on the glib rejoinder undermines your effectiveness as an orator."

Tommy smiled. He was getting somewhere. "Thanks for the tip, Monsignor, I'll be sure to remember that."

Renzulli searched for his train of thought. "If he cannot accept even one church teaching, he is not a true Catholic. This is particularly true with respect to dogma concerning faith and morals. When the pope speaks ex-cathedra about such matters, he is infallible. Ex-cathedra means—"

"I know what it means. So, of course, you apply this to the dogma concerning priests."

"Exactly."

Now they were getting to the heart of the matter, Tommy thought.

"So let's talk about papal infallibility, Monsignor Renzulli. The Catholic theologians and scholars we have interviewed for our case tell me this doctrine was not taught until 1870. If indeed the pope is infallible when he speaks on faith and morals, his infallibility didn't just start in 1870. It had to have been there, always. Why did it take so long to recognize papal infallibility if it was so obvious?"

Monsignor Renzulli just looked at him, so Tommy continued, "Those same theologians and scholars tell me that the First Vatican Council, which initiated the doctrine of papal infallibility in 1870, was convened by Pope Pius IX, who, by most accounts, was mentally unstable. On the first ballot, twenty percent of the bishops were against instituting the doctrine of papal infallibility. To be valid dogma, my experts tell me, the doctrine, whatever it is, must be divinely revealed and been taught by the Church since the time of Christ.

"The fact that 20 percent of the bishops did not agree with it initially would say that papal infallibility had not been universally taught or universally believed since the time of Christ. It took eighty-three sessions to finally reach agreement, which tells me there was plenty of dissension among the bishops with the mandate."

Monsignor Renzulli took a sip of cappuccino and put his cup down. "Almost 100 years later," he said, "the Second Vatican Council debated the issue and concurred unanimously with the mandate."

Tommy replied, "That same council also repealed what had been taught by the same Pope Pius IX. Teachings that included slavery not being at odds with the teachings of the Catholic Church and that capitalism was a sin."

"When Pius IX said those things, he was not speaking on faith and morals," Monsignor Renzulli replied firmly. "The church disagreed with what Pius IX said because he had not spoken *ex-cathedra* on faith and morals. They were merely opinions he held."

Tommy countered, "So if I understand you correctly, Monsignor, you look at what a pope says on faith and morals and choose either to believe it or not, depending upon your assessment of his state of mind when he said it? If a pope says something you agree with, then it is must be ex-cathedra, from the chair. If you don't agree with it, then it must be an *opinion?* With all due respect, Monsignor, who's the cafeteria Catholic now?"

Renzulli had heard enough. "Mr. Riley, I enjoy a good debate as much as you do. But ultimately this is pointless. If the judge sustains my motion and throws you out, that's it. If not, we will have a trial. What can you tell me about this Judge John Bateman?"

"I think you'll like him. He has a very low tolerance for the glib rejoinder."

Renzulli smiled, "And you believe he'll turn down my motion because he has a reputation as a progressive judge?"

"Your tentacles reach far and wide, Monsignor. Well done," Tommy said with relish. "No. I believe that Judge John Bateman will throw your motion out because he is intellectually curious. He's a very smart man, versed in history and philosophy as well as law. I believe he won't grant summary judgment because he won't be able to resist hearing what we've got to say. Even the most principled judge eventually grows tired of insurance fraud and workers' comp."

Tommy paused for effect. "If your motion consisted of six pages of boilerplate, yes, he might have thrown it out. But thirty-five pages of some of the best legal writing he's seen in years?" He let the words hang in the air.

Renzulli winced, "You think I overdid it."

Tommy smiled, triumphant. "Call it home-field advantage. You've got several advantages on your side. You will outspend us, guaranteed. For every witness I call, you could summon five more. The problem being, this might not see his docket for years."

Renzulli said weakly, "But that doesn't help your client resolve her case?"

Tommy pounced, "Nice try. She's got her entire life to win this case. She's young, healthy, energized. Ultra runner, apparently. Mediagenic, too, I'm sure you've noticed."

"We'll outspend you, then." Renzulli wasn't sure at what moment he had lost complete control of the conversation. "She may ultimately prevail, but we'll ruin you. We have endless resources."

"That's not going to happen." Tommy was fully in his element. "At some point, one of those Latin-speaking Italians in a bright red hat is going to send you a homing pigeon with a scroll tied to its foot and tell you to shut it down. They don't want this out there, lingering in the media, waged in the court of public opinion. They want this to go away."

Renzulli thought he saw an opening. "So that's what this is about, after all that. Very well. I can't speak on their behalf, and I myself would abhor a monetary settlement. But if it ever gets to that point, I can certainly make inquiries on your behalf."

Tommy stared back with an amused look. "Now you're boring me, Monsignor. It's beneath you. Getting on Judge Bateman's docket quickly will be problematic if we try to schedule a long trial—with discovery, witnesses, the whole nine yards."

"What do you have in mind?" Renzulli asked.

"I put on two witnesses only: Ms. Batista, plus a psychiatrist or psychologist whom the archdiocese uses to screen potential seminarians. The second witness is important because I wouldn't want to succeed in court, only to have the archdiocese disqualify Ms. Batista on a technicality."

"Has she taken the interview yet?" Renzulli asked.

"Not yet, but I'll put the examiner on, whatever their opinion. That's how confident I am that Ms. Batista is as qualified as any candidate."

"And in return?" asked Renzulli.

"You will put Archbishop Sierra on the stand. And that's it," Tommy replied.

"So you'll be relying solely upon your cross-examination of Archbishop Sierra to prove the Church's position is unreasonable. You'll have no direct testimony from expert witnesses on this issue, correct?" Monsignor Renzulli said.

"That's correct. And you will put on no expert witnesses to support his opinion. We will both tell Judge Bateman there will only be three witnesses in total. That's my proposal. That should allow for a trial, including jury selection, of two days—maybe three. With all the publicity surrounding this lawsuit,

Judge Bateman may have an incentive to find those two or three days on his docket as soon as he can," Tommy said.

"Trial by jury," Renzulli smirked. "There is a significant Catholic population in this area, counselor. Over one third."

"Let's see what the people have to say," said Tommy.

"It's a bold move, counselor," Renzulli said dubiously.

"It's the right move," Tommy replied.

Renzulli was secretly pleased. He'd had spent several nights with Jorge Sierra and had found him to be extremely intelligent and knowledgeable about the Church's position on this issue and all scriptures in general. More than that, he was humble and modest and an excellent communicator—easily relatable to potential witnesses.

"Do you know what you're up against in Jorge Sierra?" Renzulli asked.

"I've watched a few YouTube videos." Tommy Riley did not appear concerned, not in the least.

Monsignor Renzulli stood up and extended a hand to Tommy.

"It should be very interesting," Monsignor Renzulli said.

As they shook hands, Tommy asked, "Should I confirm our agreement in an e-mail?"

Monsignor Renzulli looked at him and said dryly, "Surely you can count on the word of a monsignor. I only have your word as a lawyer."

CHAPTER TWENTY-FIVE

Manuel dropped Tommy back at the office. The off-duty police officers were still there, and Tommy noticed one lonely satellite news truck clinging to a thread of hope that Tommy might grant them an interview. They were wrong. Tommy walked into the reception area. Despite it being her lunch hour, Betty was still at her desk. He wondered when she ate or slept—it seemed she was always here, no matter the time.

Ten minutes later, Silk sat across from his desk.

"He didn't even want to think about it?" Willis asked.

Tommy shook his head. "He thinks Sierra will carve me into little pieces."

"He might be right," Willis replied.

Tommy concurred, but hesitated. "Maybe, but he risks overconfidence. The jurors won't be theologians or scholars. If he gets bogged down in statutes and doctrine, he could lose them. I'll be asking questions in their terms, and he'll have to respond in theirs. If I can get him tied up in even the slightest knot, it'll be easy to convince the jury that it doesn't make sense. By the way, what's the story with Dr. Turner?"

Prentice's group had contacted and interviewed one psychiatrist and two psychologists the archdiocese used to screen applicants to the seminary. Two had declined to interview Allie and testify at trial because they did not wish to oppose the archdiocese. The third, Dr. Sylvia Turner, had readily agreed. Dr. Turner was head of the Department of Psychology at St. Thomas College. She had been selected to interview applicants to the seminary because Archbishop Sierra thought it important to have a woman's viewpoint, which might lead to a different impression of the applicants.

"All good. She told me her position is not dependent on doing work for the archdiocese. Everyone she's deemed appropriate for the seminary has been admitted. Two applicants she deemed less than ideal were ultimately turned down. She said she has the highest regard for Archbishop Sierra. Characterized him as a man of the highest integrity and morals and not always bound to the conventions of the Church. She says—are you ready for this? Sierra accepted a married Episcopal priest and ordained him into the Catholic Church."

"There are a few of those. John Paul II allowed it. Still . . . Sierra signed off?" Tommy asked.

"He did," Silk confirmed. "That being said, he is still a traditional archbishop and would certainly not do the same for a female Episcopal priest."

"Can we trust her? Dr. Turner."

"I can't see why not. She held up like a pro under my cross-examination. I don't see any bias. I believe she'll call it as she sees it," Willis answered.

"Okay, Silk, get with Allie and set up an interview with Dr. Turner. Let them both know that whatever the opinion of Dr. Turner turns out to be, it'll be presented at trial. That's my deal with Monsignor Renzulli."

"It's risky, Tommy," Willis said.

"I'm not worried. If Allie is who she—and everyone

else—says she is, she'll pass with flying colors. If she isn't, and we trust Dr. Turner to conduct a fair interview, then Allie wouldn't be admitted even if she were a male. The time to find that out is now," Tommy replied.

"Still risky," Silk said as he headed out.

CHAPTER TWENTY-SIX

At that same moment, Monsignor Renzulli was being led into the office of Archbishop Sierra. Upon entering, Sierra greeted him with a wide grin and extended a hand.

"Monsignor Renzulli, I understand you've had an eventful morning," Sierra said.

"Your Eminence," Monsignor Renzulli replied warmly.

Jorge Sierra was not an imposing man. He was of medium height with a rotund frame and looked like the grandfather everybody wished they had.

"So, what is your impression of the man?" Archbishop Sierra asked cautiously.

"He's much as you'd expect. Very opinionated. Marginal intelligence. He certainly doesn't lack confidence." Renzulli thought about it for a moment. "He's not as prepared for the case as he thinks he is. Some of his interpretations of the scriptures are totally ridiculous."

Monsignor Renzulli then explained Riley's opinion of the seventh commandment and papal infallibility.

"Creative," Archbishop Sierra said quietly. "You moved for summary judgment, I assume?"

"I did. It's pretty standard. Sometimes it even works."

"And in this case?" Archbishop Sierra asked.

"We've drawn a progressive judge. Nevertheless, I'm hopeful. We have precedent on our side; no one has sued the Church on this matter before," Renzulli said.

"Anything more to their complaint?" Sierra wondered.

Monsignor Renzulli responded, "Mr. Riley has interviewed a few theologians and scholars willing to testify that the Church's foundation for a male-only priesthood is flawed and not based on sound theology."

"That's to be expected. I assume we'll counter with our own?" Archbishop Sierra said.

Monsignor Renzulli replied, "Naturally. The problem is that a trial like this could take weeks, or even months. Judge Bateman's docket is so extended, we may not get a trial setting for two years at least."

"That might not be so bad," Archbishop Sierra said thoughtfully. "The more time it takes, the more likely the publicity will die down."

"I'm not so sure, Your Eminence," replied Renzulli. "I fear copycat lawsuits. The more cases filed, the more our chances of succeeding decrease. It's in our best interest to have this matter resolved quickly."

"I agree. How do we achieve that?" asked Archbishop Sierra.

"They benefit from a quick trial as much as we do. They have ample resources, but I can't imagine they're unlimited. Also, this Riley is aggressive by nature; he doesn't want his client waiting for a year or two. He's agreed to put on two witnesses only, Ms. Batista and one of the psychiatrists or psychologists who interview applicants for the seminary on behalf of the archdiocese. He or she will interview Miss Batista and render an opinion on her capability for the seminary, irrespective of gender," Monsignor Renzulli said.

"Why would he suggest that?" Archbishop Sierra asked.

Renzulli answered, "He wants to make sure that if he wins in court the seminary won't refuse her because she fails the review and exam. He's confident she'll pass," Monsignor Renzulli answered.

"Who picks the examiner?" the Archbishop asked.

"He will," Renzulli replied.

"We use five different examiners, and I know them all quite well," Archbishop Sierra responded. "They're all very professional and will give an objective interview to Ms. Batista. Whatever their opinion, they will tell the truth. What do we have to do in return?"

"We put on just one witness: you, Your Eminence. On direct examination and in answer to my questions, you will explain the Catholic Church's position for the male-only priesthood. After that, Riley will cross-examine you and try to punch holes in your testimony. However, he will be in your area of expertise and asking questions within your knowledge. Are you comfortable with that?" Monsignor Renzulli asked.

Archbishop Sierra thought a minute and then said quietly, "How could I not be? I have God on my side."

"Very good, Your Eminence. I have complete confidence in your testimony and, under the circumstances, I think this is an excellent deal for us."

The Archbishop put his hand on the Monsignor's shoulder. "Then let's pray, Monsignor."

The two men bowed their heads and prayed silently to the God they knew they represented on earth. They prayed that He would bestow His blessings upon His one true church.

CHAPTER TWENTY-SEVEN

John Bateman had entered his chambers, taken off his robes, and hung them in his closet. He sat down at his desk and tried to calm himself. He called for his clerk, Ashley Reed. Once she was seated, he decided it was time to vent. The young clerk was used to it; she admired the judge greatly and his clerkship was one of the most prestigious in the state.

"Doggone federal sentencing guidelines. Hogwash. We just put away one of the biggest drug dealers in the city for a whopping three years. Kids he was selling to will still be trying to pass the same grade three years from now."

"Look on the bright side," the clerk quipped. "He'll probably be back here in your courtroom before you reach senior status."

"Just no point in having it overturned because some legislator in D.C. wants to tell me how to do my job. I will not gum up the courts on an appeal. Might as well just put the judges in prison and call it a day. What else do you have for me?"

The clerk sat forward in her chair. "What are your thoughts on Batista?"

Judge Bateman produced the motion for summary judgment and the response, and waved them in front of the young clerk. "What *are* these?"

The clerk smiled. "Two powerful lawyers, each one trying to prove he has the biggest . . . gavel."

Judge Bateman laughed. He looked at the case file on the top of his desk. Both of his staff attorneys had researched the Batista case independently. He had been back and forth on whether to grant the motion and kept trying to predict how the appellate court would come down on it. He didn't want to be reversed on whatever decision he ultimately made.

"It's too close to call," he began. "If I grant the motion, then Riley will appeal and he might have a point. Gender discrimination is worthy of our utmost attention in this day and age. If I deny the motion, the Catholics will appeal; the question is, will they have grounds? In my mind, classifying priests as independent contractors gives the impression of trying to pull a fast one. What job could possibly be less independent than a Catholic priest? But of course, I must wait for the facts. Did we look into tax status?"

"The tax status of priests is complicated," the clerk began.

"Of course, it is," Bateman mused.

"Social Security considers them self-employed and the IRS considers them employees. But there are exceptions, both ways. Some take a vow of poverty, for example; others don't."

"Vow of poverty? Hogwash. Vow of poverty is when you work for minimum wage."

"Actually, some make far less than minimum wage. But at the same time, practically all of their expenses are taken care of."

"Exactly." Judge Bateman knew procrastination would only make things worse in this high-profile case and he needed to make the right decision.

"I don't want to give the impression that I'm favoring this case because it's on every doggone news show in the country."

The young law clerk thought it over for a minute. "Respectfully, Judge, this is why you build a track record of fairness—for cases like this."

"Ms. Reed, you're going to make a very persuasive attorney one day. How soon can we set up a hearing?" he asked.

His clerk studied the docket for a moment, "You have another trial set next Friday starting at 9:00 a.m. Want to delay that one?"

"What is it, remind me again?"

"Drug dealer."

"Delay it."

"Yes, Your Honor. I'll advise both parties."

"Let's make a difference before the week's out. Tell Riley and Renzulli they'll have twenty minutes each for oral arguments, and I'll put them on the clock," Judge Bateman instructed. He already felt better. The federal sentencing guidelines he could do nothing about, but the biggest media case in the country? He could certainly do something about that.

CHAPTER TWENTY-EIGHT

Tommy felt confident with the work they had done so far and decided to use his Saturday to check in with the women in his life.

He woke up early, downed an energy bar with his morning coffee, and bounced out the door with his running shoes on. Football, of course, had been the first to go; Tommy couldn't even remember the last time he had held a football. Once he turned 40, Tommy vowed to give up his usual running and occasional pick-up basketball games in favor of lower-impact sports: cycling, swimming, and rowing. The relief it gave his joints upon rising from bed each morning was immediate. Nevertheless, he was still competitive and unwilling to admit he was well past his athletic peak. So he still ran on occasion.

To reach Audubon Park and the Mississippi River Trail from his home was just about three miles. *I used to do a 5k every day before breakfast*, Tommy thought as he began to jog. But by the time he reached the Riverview, he felt the sun beating keenly down on the back of his neck and the famous humidity starting to rise. *I probably should have ridden my bike*, he thought. It was at that moment that Allie bounded up beside up.

"Great day for a run!" she smiled, running in place as Tommy slowed to a walk. "Cooler than usual."

"Is it?" he responded.

"Are you ready?"

"Of course I'm ready," Tommy replied. And off they went.

"I usually run to Kenner," said Allie. "But this is a decent warm-up."

"Kenner? Isn't that 20 miles along the trail?" Tommy asked.

"Twenty-two," she replied.

"How do you get back? Do you have someone pick you up?"

Allie laughed. "No, I run back."

"So you're a marathoner," Tommy panted.

"I do run marathons, yes, but it's not my best distance. The longer the race, the better I finish. From 50 to 100—that's when I really hit my stride."

"100 kilometers?" Tommy stopped running.

"Sure," said Allie, jogging in place. "100 kilometers. 100 miles."

"You've run 100 miles?!" Tommy was in disbelief.

"Many times," said Allie. They had only run a short distance when she motioned for them to sit on a nearby park bench.

"An ultra-marathoner," Tommy stated, once he had finally caught his breath.

"Ultra, yes. Do you know the Bandera races?" she asked.

"In the Texas Hill Country? Of course. You wouldn't know it from my performance today, but I ran there in 2004. 25 kilometers, obviously. So you ran the 100?" Tommy was growing more in awe of Allie every day.

"I won it! Not that year, but last year."

"How long does it take?" Tommy inquired.

"My whole life," Allie replied.

"I mean, to run the race."

"I know what you meant. Nine or ten hours."

Tommy suddenly felt sheepish. He was used to being the sports hero. "Well, I was probably one of the people you passed on the way to the finish."

"The distance you choose isn't important. What's important is finishing the distance."

Even though his cells were still sapped of strength, her words weren't lost on Tommy.

"I've got your back, Allie, all the way to the end. I'm very optimistic. But even if this first time in court doesn't go the way we want, we still have other options. Appeals. Other venues. I'm with you on this, all the way to the finish."

"What if there is no finish line?"

Tommy looked at her and realized she was serious. He wanted to believe in her. He truly did.

Tommy realized he had to leave for a date with Nikki. Tommy was finally ready to admit to himself that a boozy brunch was a better way to spend his Saturday than trying to keep up with an elite distance runner.

"Well," he finally said. "We'll cross that bridge when we come to it."

†

He met Nikki at the Columns Hotel on St. Charles Avenue. Having a meal outdoors while overlooking the famed streetcar line was a local tradition, and Tommy had been going there since he was a little boy. As such, he exempted it from his short list of local watering holes.

Nikki was wearing perfectly distressed jeans with a loose linen top and gold and wooden jewelry. She would have looked equally at home at a beach bar on the French

Riviera, or on an African safari. Tommy was just happy to be seated with her on one of the most notable patios in New Orleans.

She had ordered his customary Ramos Gin Fizz, and had already finished her own. Tommy noticed wryly that it may not have been her first.

"Sorry I'm late," he said, giving her a peck on the cheek. "I had a meeting with a client."

"You went for a run with a runner," was Nikki's retort. "A running client."

Tommy was surprised until she pointed at his running shoes. He had changed quickly and had absentmindedly put his running shoes back on.

"You only wear those ugly things when you go for a run. And you haven't gone for a run in years."

Tommy laughed. "A running client. Guilty."

Just then a server stopped by with a tray. "Who ordered the double?" he asked.

Nikki raised her hand. "Right here."

Tommy smiled. "A double? Easy tiger."

Nikki inhaled her drink deeply through a straw. "I don't have to be in court Monday. And I can drink you under the table and you know it."

Tommy motioned to clink glasses. "A point I will not argue, counselor."

Nikki finished the rest of her drink and motioned for another. "Don't you think it's a little weird to be going for a run on a Saturday morning with a client when you're due in court two days later? A little unprofessional?"

"Not at all," he replied quickly. "This is not going to be easy on her. I wanted to be absolutely certain this is something she's up for."

"I'm not worried about her. I think you want to be sure that you're up for this."

Tommy knew better than to argue with Nikki when she had had a few too many. What little she lost in brainpower she gained in pure tenaciousness.

"I'm just a gun-for-hire counselor. Don't worry about me."

"That's what I'm worried about. You don't take these cases for the money. You do it because somewhere deep down in that chest where your heart is supposed to be, you do it because you care. Why do you care about this one? Is it her?"

Tommy felt the ground shift under his feet. "If I didn't know you better, Ms. Butler, I'd say you were jealous."

Nikki sighed derisively. "I'm not even going to honor that with a protest, lest you think I protest too much. So put it out of your head. She's beautiful. And she's a nun. Moving on."

Now Tommy was confused. "So why are you worried about me taking the case?"

"Why am I worried?" Nikki's voice rose as another drink was served. "I should have been worried the other night with your religious ramblings, but you were too damn charming to object. I'm not a religious person. But you clearly have childhood issues that you have not resolved."

"Nikki, not at all. I just enjoy a spirited debate. That's it."

"But your mother? You're all she has. And you're going to risk never speaking to her again over this case?"

"Nikki," Tommy tried.

"Don't Nikki me!" Her volume caused most if not all of the patio to turn in their direction, before normal conversation slowly resumed.

As Tommy stared at Nikki, he quickly realized two things. He realized that he loved this woman he was sitting with, and that he wanted to sit with her for the rest of his life. And he also realized that he wanted to win Allie's case more than ever before.

Finally, he smiled wide and said, "Mr. Churchill, I do believe you're drunk." An old, familiar routine they had adopted.

Nikki took his hand and smiled back. "Lady Astor, I may be drunk but tomorrow I will be sober. And you will still be ugly."

†

Tommy skipped his afternoon visit with Luisa that day. With arguments due in court Monday morning and an exhausting morning with two of the women in his life, he needed a mental break. Besides, he wasn't so sure Luisa was ready to see him.

CHAPTER TWENTY-NINE

When Manuel pulled up to the courthouse, the news outlets were out in full force—reporters and cameramen standing two deep. Tommy had suspected this might be the most well-attended docket hearing in Orleans Parish in a long while, and this crush of people seemed to prove him right. But even he was surprised by the showing. If he was going to get through the chaos in a timely manner, and more importantly stay focused on the matter he was bringing to Judge Batmen in a matter of minutes, he'd need a diversion.

"Manny, may I use your phone and headphones?" Tommy requested.

"Sure thing, Mr. Riley," Manuel answered, and didn't bother to ask why. Such was the nature of Manny's loyalty.

"What kind of music?" Manuel asked.

"Surprise me. Something to get me in the mood," Tommy answered.

Manuel found a selection and smiled, handing Tommy the phone.

"This should get your blood pumping," Manuel said. "Good luck, boss."

Tommy exited the car to the beat of Colombian Salsa, a smooth and surprisingly perfect soundtrack for the chaos he confronted. He walked ahead with a smile on his face, oblivious to anything but his destination ahead. Inside, he pushed through another wave of reporters, finally entering the calm of the courtroom. Removing the headphones, Tommy was struck by just how quiet it was. Appropriately enough, it reminded him of a church. The courtroom also had reporters already seated, but they knew better than to yell questions. Instead they were here to record the show. Tommy noticed no cameras were in the courtroom and guessed that Judge Bateman had prohibited them. No surprises there.

He took his seat at the plaintiff's table and looked across the aisle at his opponents. Monsignor Renzulli dressed in the black suit of a priest with a white Roman collar, wearing none of the purple designating his rank of monsignor. Seated next to him was the young priest who had escorted him to Renzulli's office at the archdiocese. Also seated at the table were a man and a woman whom Tommy recognized as local counsel. Tommy nodded to Monsignor Renzulli, and he nodded back. Game on.

At 9:00 a.m. the bailiff announced, "All rise," and Judge Bateman climbed the steps to his bench.

Judge Bateman said, "We're here in the matter of Alejandra Batista versus the Archdiocese of New Orleans and Archbishop Jorge Sierra. On the docket this morning is a hearing on the motion for summary judgment duly filed by the defendants. Is the counsel for the plaintiff present and ready?"

"We are, Your Honor," Tommy stood and said.

"Is counsel for the defendants present and ready?"

"We are, Your Honor," Monsignor Renzulli likewise answered. "The court has received the motion and brief in support thereof from the defendants, and the response and a brief in support thereof from the plaintiff," Judge Bateman said. "The court will allow twenty minutes of oral argument from each side. Monsignor, since it's your motion, you're up and you're on the clock."

CHAPTER THIRTY

Monsignor Renzulli stood up. "Your Honor, our position is stated quite simply. The plaintiff is attempting to insert the government into the defendants' ecclesiastical rules, which has no precedent in American law."

Before he could continue, Judge Bateman interrupted. "Monsignor Renzulli, are you suggesting that because a certain set of facts has never been reviewed before by a court that the court has no power to review those facts as they pertain to existing law?"

"Not at all, Your Honor," Monsignor Renzulli answered. "What I'm suggesting is that this set of facts, this cause of action, has not been reviewed before because it's clear that no court has jurisdiction over the ecclesiastical rules of any church, as it is clearly prohibited by the First Amendment. No action of this kind would have been initiated by anyone with a fundamental knowledge of United States constitutional law. Under the First Amendment, it's clear that the state, or a court on its behalf, may not intrude into the internal activities of a religious association or church."

"Monsignor Renzulli, my staff attorneys have researched recent sex-scandal cases against the Catholic Church, and a large number of courts have ruled they have jurisdiction over those activities, despite similar First Amendment arguments to the contrary. What is the difference here?" Judge Bateman asked.

"Your Honor, those cases involve misconduct by a very small number of priests. The church became involved in litigation due to activities by certain bishops of the Church after they discovered misconduct by one or more priests. The bishops involved meant well, but those activities were not official dogma or teaching of the Catholic Church," Monsignor Renzulli answered.

"So is it your position that the court has legal jurisdiction over unofficial activities of your church, but not over official activities of your church? If an unofficial activity is against the law and the court has jurisdiction, why wouldn't a court likewise have jurisdiction when an official activity is allegedly against the law?" Judge Bateman asked.

"The fundamental difference is that those unofficial activities were not an essential part of the religion of the Catholic Church. The cases you mention were based upon the alleged negligence of certain bishops and their actions after they discovered misconduct and how they handled the situations. The activities involved in those cases were not part of the religious doctrine of the Catholic Church, and therefore the guarantee of the freedom of religion does not apply to activities that are not part of the religious doctrine. What is at stake here is a fundamental and basic tenet of the Catholic religion, and precisely that which the First Amendment guarantees the people of this country to believe and practice," Monsignor Renzulli argued.

Judge Bateman responded, "That is your argument—even if the protection of that freedom under the First Amendment would cause the infringement of the rights of the plaintiff, who also has equal protection of the law to her rights?"

"Your Honor," Monsignor Renzulli answered, "Ms. Batista's rights arise out of legislation, and I submit that whenever an enacted law conflicts with the Constitution, the Constitution is controlling, and that legislation is unconstitutional."

"Then is it your opinion that the Civil Rights Act is unconstitutional?" Judge Bateman asked.

"No, Your Honor, not the act. But the application of the act under the facts in this instance would be," Monsignor Renzulli answered.

"Do you have anything else, Monsignor?" Judge Bateman asked.

"No, Your Honor," Renzulli said.

Turning to Tommy, Judge Bateman said, "Mr. Riley, it's your turn, and you are now on the clock."

"Your Honor, I will also be brief," Tommy started. "What we have here is a well-settled law that states that no one, and I emphasize no one, can discriminate against a woman solely because of her gender without justifiable cause. There is no question at all that the Catholic Church is discriminating against women by allowing only, and I quote, 'unmarried males who have been baptized and confirmed in the Catholic Church' to a Catholic seminary. That is discrimination on its face.

"Do they have justifiable reason for that? The defendants claim that the First Amendment prohibits an examination of that issue. We vehemently disagree. Say, for example, a church, as a basic tenet of its religion and as an official activity, practiced human sacrifice. Could anyone reasonably say that this court could not review that practice under United States law?"

Before Tommy could continue, Judge Bateman interrupted and asked, "Mr. Riley, human sacrifice would be the murder of another human being and would be a felonious crime. Are you suggesting that the Catholic Church is undertaking criminal activities in not allowing your client admission to the seminary?"

"No. Your Honor, what they're doing is, on its face, a violation of civil law. Is a civil law less valid than a criminal law? Federal courts have assumed jurisdiction over the Church in violation of civil law in the cases which Your Honor previously mentioned and over other churches as well. For example, federal courts assumed jurisdiction over The Church of Latter Day Saints, also known as Mormons, concerning their religious right of polygamy. The courts ruled the civil laws against polygamy outweighed the Church's right to the practice under the First Amendment. There is no difference here. The court should assume jurisdiction over the defendants in this case, and they should be required to prove their treatment of women is not discriminatory under the law. They should be required to prove they have justifiable cause to discriminate. The First Amendment does not protect them from this obligation," Tommy finished.

"Are you finished, Mr. Riley?" Judge Bateman asked.

"Just one more point, Your Honor. I believe it's important to look at what the framers of the Constitution had in mind when they wrote the First Amendment. They had just successfully won their independence from England, a country that at the time required all citizens to belong to the Church of England. The framers wanted all citizens to have the right to practice the religion of their choice, not to have a single religion dictated by the state. That's it.

"It goes without saying that those men did not intend that a constitutional right would protect *illegal* activity. It was to protect *legitimate* activity. To do otherwise would be, in my opinion, a violation of due process. The defendants should be required to explain the reasons for their actions to a judge and jury, who would then determine whether those actions constitute legitimate activity or not. Now I'm finished, Your Honor." Tommy said.

"Do you have any rebuttal, Monsignor?" Judge Bateman asked.

"Yes, Your Honor," Monsignor Renzulli said as he stood up at his table. "Plaintiff's counsel has raised the intent of those who drafted the Constitution and has suggested that it was not intended to protect illegal activity. I will agree, as I'm sure most people would with that statement. But let's look at the activity in question here. The Catholic Church was a predominant religion at the time the Constitution was drafted, and the male-only priesthood was a well-known fact. If they did not intend the First Amendment to protect an existing and well-known activity of any religion prevalent at the time, whether it was Quaker, Presbyterian, Lutheran, or Catholic, they would have made an exception. Obviously they didn't.

"I think it's important to also note that of the first ten amendments in the Bill of Rights, this is the first one. It only seems logical that what they felt was most important would be listed first. This amendment must supersede any subsequent legislation. *Freedom* means just that, Your Honor. The right to do as one wishes without restrictions.

"Now, Your Honor, I'm also finished," Monsignor Renzulli said.

"Any counter rebuttal, Mr. Riley?"

"Well since Your Honor is kind enough to ask, yes. Let me just remind the court that when the Bill of Rights was written, women did not have the right to vote, they did not have the right to serve in the military, they had limited rights to property, and were barely protected—if at all—from sexual abuse and workplace discrimination."

"Anything else Mr. Riley?" Judge Bateman sighed.

"Absolutely. As an officer of the court, I feel compelled to mention that our fair neighbor, the great state of Mississippi, did not even allow women to sit on a jury until 1968! Your Honor, the Founding Fathers, visionaries all, were still fallible when it came to projecting human rights 200 years into the future. Thank you."

Judge Bateman stared at Tommy as if he wanted to say something but finally decided it wasn't worth the trouble. So he turned to the Monsignor. "Mr. Renzulli, may I assume that everything of value concerning this matter has already been said."

"You may, Your Honor," said Renzulli.

"Well, in that case, the court is ready to rule on the motion," Judge Bateman said.

The courtroom became eerily quiet.

CHAPTER THIRTY-ONE

Judge Bateman began, "Our forefathers drafted some of the most poignant language in human history when they said, 'All men are created equal.' Unfortunately, when they coined those words, they didn't mean men of color, because most of the signatories were slave owners themselves. Therefore, when courts centuries later looked at the purpose of those words to define whether it applied to issues before them, any court bound by the framers' intent could not apply it to men of color.

"Eventually, judges had the opportunity to review those words in consideration of their present day, and not in light of the times in which the words were drafted. Although the original purpose was not to include black men as equal to and being afforded the same rights as white men, judges nevertheless overturned the original intent and took the step to interpret those words to include all men of color. They set a precedent that was followed by other courts, which led to legislation that specifically included all men of color, the Civil Rights Act of 1964. That legislation also accomplished something that our forefathers also did not expressly denote: it included women as well. At the time of the Constitution, women in this country could not vote, own land, obtain a divorce, sign a legal document, or be educated beyond elementary school. They obviously were not intended to have the same rights as men by the framers of the Constitution. But today, all men and women of whatever color or creed have the same rights under the laws of this country. That is very clear.

"Monsignor Renzulli has argued this court has no jurisdiction over the defendants in this case, since their right to practice their religion under the First Amendment prohibits *any* interference by the government in that freedom. However, other courts have found jurisdiction over this same church when the activities of their church violated the laws of this country. The defendants argue that this is different, in that those activities were not officially sanctioned, nor were they part of the doctrine of their church.

"However, the defendants readily admit they only allow men to qualify for the seminary, and I have to assume they believe they have justifiable cause to do so.

"The plaintiff has argued forcibly in her brief that a seminary is an institution of higher learning and has cited several cases where courts have ruled to allow women into institutions of higher learning when, prior to the ruling, those institutions were restricted to males. This court does take notice that none of those particular cases involves the First Amendment right to freedom of religion. The plaintiff has also argued that the rights of one person, or entity, should not be protected when that protection creates undue harm under the law to the legal rights of another. However, the defendants have argued that the protection of the rights of the plaintiff creates undue harm to their own legal rights, and their rights under the Constitution supersede her rights under legislation.

"In summary, this court is being asked to balance the conflicting legal rights of the parties involved in this lawsuit and determine which way the scales of justice tilt. To begin with, this court is persuaded that other courts have taken jurisdiction over the activities of the Church involved in this case. This court is also persuaded that there is a basic fact question here over the activities of this church in this action. Do the defendants have justifiable cause to exclude women from the seminary, an institution of higher learning? Since there is ample precedent to assume jurisdiction over the defendants and a fact question exists, I hereby overrule the motion for summary judgment. I am prepared to schedule this for trial," Judge Bateman finished.

Bingo, Tommy thought. He would take fifty-fifty any time.

†

Tommy heard the shuffling of people leaving the courtroom, no doubt reporters eager to get on camera and report this breaking news first.

Monsignor Renzulli immediately stood up and said, "Your Honor, we take exception to your ruling as a matter of law."

"Duly noted, Monsignor Renzulli," Judge Bateman replied.

"We also move for a stay in these proceedings so that we may file an appeal to the United States appellate court. If the appellate court should find in our favor, then this court and both parties would save the costs and time to try this case," Monsignor Renzulli argued.

"Motion to stay proceedings overruled; exception also noted," Judge Bateman said. He then turned to Tommy and said, "Mr. Riley, you have requested a jury trial. Is that correct?"

Judge Bateman had the right to grant his request for a jury trial or not. If he did not grant the request, the question of justifiable reason of the defendants' actions would be solely Judge Bateman's to determine. He would also have the sole discretion to determine whether an injunction to allow Allie into the seminar was in order. It was a lot of power in the hands of one person—a scenario Tommy wished to avoid.

"We have, Your Honor," Tommy replied.

"You recognize that this court will have the right to determine whether a mandatory injunction is justified, even if the jury sides with your client?" Judge Bateman asked.

"Yes, Your Honor," Tommy responded. He understood that the judge would have the final say on whether the Church would be required to admit her to the seminary.

"What is your request, Mr. Riley, regarding the size of the jury? Do you want a six-person or twelve-person jury?" Judge Bateman asked.

"Your Honor, the plaintiff requests a six-person jury," Tommy answered.

"Is there any specific reason you have requested six jurors and not twelve?" Judge Bateman asked.

Silk and Tommy had discussed the odds in detail. While either men or women might be sympathetic to Allie's case, having a single, traditional Catholic capable of articulating their views in the jury room might prove fatal to their case. They decided that the smaller the jury, the easier it would be keep out potential roadblocks. Tommy did not explain his true rationale to Judge Bateman, however, but said instead, "Your Honor, a smaller jury will require less time for jury selection and shorten the time needed on your docket."

After a moment or two of thought, Judge Bateman said, "The court grants the plaintiff's request for a six-person jury.

Now let's talk about a trial setting. Neither party has requested discovery, which is highly unusual. Is that still the position of the parties?"

"Yes, Your Honor," Tommy said.

"It is, Your Honor," Monsignor Renzulli said.

"How many witnesses do you plan to call, Mr. Riley?" Judge Bateman asked.

"Your Honor, I have made an agreement with Monsignor Renzulli. I will call two witnesses, and he will call one witness. That's it."

Judge Bateman was stunned. In all his years on the bench, this was a first. He asked, "What is your estimate of time of trial, Mr. Riley?"

Tommy answered, "Two days."

"Monsignor Renzulli?"

Monsignor replied, "The same, Your Honor."

Judge Bateman turned to his law clerk and asked, "When can we have trial setting for a two-day duration?"

Ashley Reed replied, "Your Honor, you had a trial set for four days beginning next Tuesday, but the parties notified the court yesterday that it had been settled. We could do it then if Your Honor would like."

"In that case, trial is set for 9:00 a.m. next Tuesday. Are there any questions?"

There were none.

CHAPTER THIRTY-TWO

The moment the Judge sent the case to trial, Michel stood up with disgust. Even though he stood up slowly, the blood still rushed from his head and he felt faint, causing him to grab the bench in front of him. His stomach churned and twisted with torment, and he knew that he would have to act or it would never go away. He surveyed the chaos in the courtroom.

In Michel's twisted vision, it was another sign of the Apocalypse. The condescending Judge Bateman profaned the Church with every word. His lack of respect was grounds for recusal, but still he persisted in his mockery. The fate of the entire Church would potentially rest in the hands of six non-believers. Michel would have to take matters into his own hands if the situation didn't improve. His superiors had made that very clear.

CHAPTER THIRTY-THREE

Tuesday morning, Manuel dropped Tommy, Silk, Allie, and Dr. Turner off at the back of the federal building. Since he was as eager to avoid the media circus as they were, Judge Bateman had arranged for all parties to use his private entrance. Jury selection was often a long-winded affair and he wanted no delays.

A few days earlier, Tommy had interviewed Dr. Turner who informed him that Allie had passed the psychological exam with flying colors. Tommy wasn't surprised in the least, but it still came as a welcome relief. Tommy had spent a morning with Dr. Turner to go over her report and the questions he would ask her on the stand. He'd also spent hours with Allie, practicing direct testimony and, more importantly, the cross-examination that Renzulli and his team would unleash when it was their turn. Tommy thought she was as prepared as any client he'd ever had.

As the team entered the room, murmurs from the back of the house announced Allie's appearance. Other than her DMV headshot, and the old yearbook pictures that some reporters had unearthed, this was the first time the press had seen Alejandra Batista. Tommy could hear the artists jostling to get a better view for their sketches of his client.

Tommy had assumed Allie cared little for her outward appearance, but the more time he spent with her the more he realized that her effortless style was carefully cultivated. Her hair was neatly trimmed into a bob and her bangs, usually windblown, were perfectly coiffed. Her ballerina flats made her seem more demure than usual, and she topped skinny dark pants with a long sleeve cotton navy blouse. She smiled at the press just as they had rehearsed, making brief eye contact with each of the network-news reporters. But as Tommy watched her survey the room, he realized that no amount of practice could produce her serene self-confidence.

Tommy looked over to the defendants' table and noted one major addition since the hearing: Archbishop Jorge Sierra. He was dressed in a simple black suit with a white Roman collar, not the excessive robes and hat of an archbishop. It was a shrewd move by the defense team, making Sierra seem down to earth in the eyes of the jurors. It seemed that each side shared the common goal of making their principal witness seem more friendly and less intimidating.

At 9:00 a.m., the bailiff intoned "all rise" and members of the courtroom stood to their feet. "The United States District Court for the Eastern District of Louisiana is now in session on the matter of Alejandra Batista versus the Archdiocese of New Orleans, the honorable Judge John Bateman presiding."

Judge Bateman said, "Bailiff, will you please escort the jury panel in and have them seated by number?"

The bailiff returned minutes later with forty people. A questionnaire had been sent to all prospective jurors who had been subpoenaed for that week. The forty who made up the panel had been picked at random. Both counsel received copies of the questionnaire with the responses submitted by each of the members of the jury panel.

Other than the usual questions—name, occupation, address, and any history with litigation—Judge Bateman posed an additional question that Tommy had requested. It simply asked a yes or no question, "Are you a practicing Catholic?" To Tommy's mild surprise, Monsignor Renzulli had not objected. Sixteen of the forty people on the jury panel answered *yes*.

Jurors were selected in numerical order, so the first fifteen were very important to both Tommy and Monsignor Renzulli. Each had three preemptory challenges they could use to excuse potential jurors for any reason, which would leave nine remaining. There were also unlimited challenges for cause, which they could use on a juror whose answers to questions showed a bias for one side or the other. Judge Bateman, however, would have to agree with the challenge. Assuming both Tommy and Monsignor Renzulli used their preemptory objections, and there were no exceptions for cause, the first six would serve on the jury, and the next three would serve as alternates, if Judge Bateman desired. If any of the nine were excused, then number ten would be seated, and so on down the line. At the request of the judge, the bailiff swore in the forty prospective jurors.

The jury listened intently as Judge Bateman gave his instructions. "You're being asked to sit on the case of Alejandra Batista versus the Archdiocese of New Orleans and Archbishop Jorge Sierra. I will ask you a series of questions first, then the attorneys will ask you a series of questions under what is known as "voir dire." The purpose of these questions is to elicit your answers under oath and determine whether you can be an impartial juror, listen to the testimony of all witnesses objectively, and render a fair and impartial decision. Does anybody have a question about the process?"

After a brief silence with no response, Judge Bateman continued, "Other than those of you who are Catholic and would be part of the archdiocese, do any of you personally know Alejandra Batista or Archbishop Jorge Sierra?"

Again, with no response from the jury, Judge Bateman probed further. "Does any one of you know either Thomas Patrick Riley, counsel for the plaintiff, or Monsignor Renzulli, counsel for the defendants?" Two people raised their hands, and after questioning by Judge Bateman they said that Mr. Riley had represented close family members. They were excused, and the panel shrank to 38.

Judge Bateman cautioned the jury further. "This case has received a great amount of attention in the media. Have any of you, by way of news reports or any other sources, formed an opinion about this case one way or the other? Remember, you are under oath." Eighteen people raised their hands, twelve of whom had answered the questionnaire as being Catholic. Judge Bateman excused all eighteen without asking their opinion. They were now down to twenty, Tommy thought—still enough for a quorum. Best of all, only four Catholics remained.

Clearing his throat, Judge Bateman continued, "Of the rest of you, how many have read newspaper accounts or watched TV news reports about this lawsuit?" Everyone raised their hands except for one small, older man with a thoughtful expression—juror number fifteen. Tommy wondered where he had been the last month. How did he miss this story in the headlines?

Judge Bateman continued, "Those of you who have raised your hands, will the news reports you have either read or heard influence your decision in any way in this case? If so, please raise your hand." No one did.

"You will hear sworn testimony from witnesses over the next two days, which could very well conflict with what has been reported in news accounts. You will be sworn to ignore what you have heard before today. Is there anyone who will have a difficult time doing this? If so, please raise your hand." Again, no one did.

Satisfied he had an impartial jury panel, Judge Bateman glanced at the clock and said, "It's close to noon. We will recess for lunch. Jurors, you will go with the bailiff to the cafeteria in the basement. You are instructed to stay together and not to talk to anyone unless they are on this jury panel. You may talk amongst yourselves about anything you wish but *not* about this case. Is that clear?" Each prospective juror nodded in the affirmative.

Judge Bateman continued, "For those of you who will be selected for the jury to hear testimony in this case, those will be your instructions until you are dismissed."

Glancing at the clock again, Judge Bateman continued, "Court will be adjourned until 1:30."

†

After lunch, Tommy began. He concentrated on the remaining Catholics, inquiring about their bias for or against a woman priest. Not surprisingly, during *his* "voir dire," Monsignor Renzulli left the Catholics alone and concentrated on the women and their affiliations with pro-feminist groups. The questioning by both counsels took up most of the afternoon, with panel members being excused either peremptorily or for cause.

The first six in order of the remaining numbers included two women and four men, one of the men being Catholic. The final panel would have included two Catholics, except that

Tommy had challenged one juror for cause when he asked if he would have a problem going to Mass and Communion presided over by a woman priest.

When the juror answered, "I don't know. How can I call her Father?" Judge Bateman granted the challenge.

Upon questioning, the small, older man volunteered that he was of the Hindu religion. Tommy shot Silk a questioning look which was returned with a shrug that meant, "Why not? At least he's not Catholic."

As five o'clock approached, Judge Bateman decided to wrap things up. They had their jury panel. "Members of the jury, the bailiff will instruct you as to the selection of your foreperson. We will hear opening arguments tomorrow morning." With that he banged the gavel and adjourned the court until the nine o'clock the following morning.

As Tommy and Willis were leaving the courtroom, Tommy asked, "Silk—Hindus. What do we know?"

"Not much. Vague notions at best. Predates Christianity, and by a lot. But more traditional, less traditional—no idea."

"Me either. That's our homework tonight then," Tommy replied.

CHAPTER THIRTY-FOUR

On Wednesday morning, Tommy made his opening statement. He was brief and to the point.

"The evidence will clearly show that the plaintiff, Alejandra Batista, is in every way an appropriate candidate to enter the seminary and study for the priesthood. The only qualification she lacks is that the Catholic Church requires her to be of the male gender. There will be no dispute about this. The only question of fact that you, the jury, must determine is whether the defendants have justifiable cause to discriminate against her because she happens to be born of the female gender.

"The evidence will also show that the Catholic Church professes that it is the first church established by Jesus Christ. The evidence will further show that the defendants will rely not on what Jesus Christ did, said, or taught—but rather, what Jesus Christ did not do, say, or teach—in order to justify their position of gender discrimination. Their entire underlying premise is that Jesus Christ did not name women as apostles 2,000 years ago, and so he therefore meant to exclude women forever from the Catholic clergy. There are many reasons why Jesus Christ acted as he did, none of which sought to forever deny women the right to be priests, and the evidence will show this. Once you see and understand the evidence presented to you, you will have no choice but to end gender discrimination and find for the plaintiff."

Monsignor Renzulli was equally concise.

"This great country was founded upon the bedrock of religious freedom. The Founding Fathers separated church and state for a reason: so that every religion could practice according to the dictates of their beliefs. The Jewish faith practices according to their beliefs. The Islamic religion is accorded a wide berth in our courts and our society to worship as they see fit. There is no reason that a Christian religion—Baptist, Presbyterian, or in this case Catholic—should not be afforded that same respect.

"The evidence will show the defendants follow their scriptures as they believe to be correct, and as the sacred Word of God. It will further show that for two thousand years since the time of Christ, the Catholic Church has been consistent in their interpretation of the scriptures. It will also show that the Catholic Church does not discriminate against women and that women are given a special place of honor in the Church.

"The evidence will also show that the teaching of the male-only priesthood is, in the eyes of the Church, the will of God. It follows the example of Jesus Christ. The Church could not change this doctrine even if it wanted to. The preponderance of evidence will show that the defendants do not discriminate against women by the doctrine of a male-only priesthood. It's the only logical result based upon the Church's religious teaching, and as such, the only choice you will have is to find for the defendants."

Judge Bateman then asked Tommy to call his first witness. "Your Honor, we call Alejandra Batista to the stand," Tommy said.

†

A murmur resonated from the back of the courtroom as Alejandra Batista left the plaintiff's table and walked to the witness stand. Tommy did not waste time.

"Ms. Batista, did you apply to the Roman Catholic Archdiocese of New Orleans to attend the seminary in its jurisdiction?" he began.

"Yes, I did."

"Did they accept your application?"

"No," she paused for emphasis, "they did not."

"Did they tell you why they did not accept your application?"

"I was told I did not meet the basic qualifications for an applicant to the seminary," Allie answered.

"What are the basic qualifications for being an applicant to the seminary?" Tommy asked.

"An applicant must be baptized and confirmed in the Catholic Church, and be a non-married male," Allie replied.

"And have you been baptized and confirmed in the Catholic church, Ms. Batista?"

"Yes. And I have been a faithful adherent of the Catholic Church my entire life."

"Ms. Batista, are you married or have you ever been married?"

"No, Mr. Riley, I'm not married and I have never been married," Alejandra said firmly.

"What is your gender, Ms. Batista?" Tommy asked.

"I was born female, and I identify as female."

"So, if I understand you correctly, you fulfill the qualifications of being unmarried, as well as baptized and confirmed in the Catholic Church. Is that correct?"

"Yes, Mr. Riley."

"And the only reason your application to attend the seminary was denied is because you are not a male. Is that correct?"

Monsignor Renzulli interjected, "Objection, Your Honor, the question calls for an answer that is not within her scope of knowledge."

"Sustained," Judge Bateman ruled.

Tommy recovered quickly. "I'll rephrase the question. To the best of your knowledge, are there any reasons you would be denied admittance to the seminary, other than being a woman?" Tommy asked Allie.

"No, Mr. Riley."

"Ms. Batista, why do you want to be a priest?"

Alejandra's voice was soft and feminine but filled with conviction. Just as Tommy had taught her, she looked earnestly at the jury.

"I want to be a priest because I believe it is my calling in life, and it's something I have felt since I was very young. When I was asked what I wanted to be when I grew up, as all children are, I would always say a priest. Everyone would laugh, so I learned to keep my destiny to myself. But as I grew older, the calling became stronger. I know I have the spirituality, the desire to help others, and the dedication to do God's work."

"How does the position of the Church make you feel?" Tommy asked quietly.

Allie gazed out at the packed courtroom. "Frustrated. Because I am unable to develop my full potential."

"Why don't you just accept your fate, as countless others have?"

"If I was more accepting of my fate, none of these people would be here today." She smiled at Judge Bateman. "Except for you, Your Honor."

As polite laughter filled the courtroom, Renzulli grew im-patient. "Objection, witness is . . ." he grasped for something he couldn't quite verbalize.

"Overruled," said Judge Bateman. "Her answer is factually correct. But you made your point. Ms. Batista, please stick to the matter at hand."

"You are a Sister of the Church, correct? You have taken the vows of a nun?"

"Yes."

"And does that fulfill your lifelong dream?"

"It does not."

"And how is that, Ms. Batista? You attend the same services as the priests. You minister to the same congregations."

"First, let me state that the work of the Sisters worldwide is of the utmost importance. I have nothing but respect and reverence for the work that they—that we—do. But I was called to be a priest. I was called to deliver the Mass and the Eucharist and the Sacraments directly to the people. I cannot serve the people in this way as a nun. My only wish is to serve the people in the greatest capacity possible."

"Let's get back to the gender requirement of the Church. In your mind, what constitutes the definition of a male human being? Or female, for that matter."

"I have learned that it isn't always as well-defined as people think. It's very confusing for some individuals. For most, it's a combination of chromosomes, hormones, personality, and, of course, genitalia."

"Is there any role for male genitalia in priestly functions that you know of?"

The courtroom erupted in nervous snickers and Monsignor Renzulli rose to his feet.

"Objection, Your Honor."

"Sustained. Mr. Riley, I'm warning you. We are here for a specific reason. Please stick to it."

Riley turned to the Judge. "Your Honor, the specific discrimination here is gender based; we need to discuss all aspects of what that means."

Judge Bateman appeared to waver. "Monsignor Renzulli?"

"Your Honor, as we all know, my organization has been embroiled in a completely unrelated matter that has ruined many lives and cost millions of dollars. But as the gender directive for a male-only priesthood predates the current matter by several centuries, asking if 'male genitalia have a role in priestly functions' is irrelevant. Not to mention rude, sacrilegious, and, quite frankly, insulting."

"Mr. Riley?"

"Your Honor, Monsignor Renzulli's point that the Catholic priest sex-abuse scandal is irrelevant is obvious, point granted. But since he brought it up, can we at least consider the fact that well over 90% of sex offenders are male, and that maybe their little 'difficulty' could have been avoided by allowing female priests?"

The courtroom exploded like a volcano. A few of the younger visitors let out whoops and shouts.

"You two! Approach the bench!"

Judge Bateman's eyeglasses started to fog up and he snapped them off his head. By the time he spoke, he was perfectly calm.

"We discussed a very specific scenario to get you on the docket and I will not have that agreement abrogated. Do you hear me? No showboating, no shenanigans. Understood?"

The men nodded in unison. Judge Bateman lowered his voice.

"If I have to go on Paxil again because of you two clowns, I will never, ever forgive you. You won't see me lose my cool.

All you will see is the inside of a cell, and I will have you waterboarded so help me God. Now rephrase the question."

As the men skulked back, Judge Bateman turned to the panel. "The jury will please wipe the preceding five minutes from your collective minds. It shall not factor into your deliberations, understood? Mr. Riley."

Tommy resumed. "Where were we? Ms. Batista, does the requirement of maleness as you define it, chromosomes, hormones"—he glanced cautiously at the Judge—"and genitalia make any sense to you as a job requirement for the priesthood?"

"No," she said, looking back at the jury. "Priests take a vow of celibacy, so they are effectively neutered in that sense."

"Is there a job requirement of strength or physical power, as we have seen overturned in cases involving the military and law enforcement?"

Allie smiled, "Other than bearing the weight of men's souls, no. There is no need for physical strength."

Tommy glanced at the jury. She was charming their pants off just as he had suspected.

"You mentioned a calling. Do you know if God is calling you to the priesthood?" Tommy asked.

"Objection, Your Honor!" Monsignor Renzulli interrupted again. "She cannot possibly know what's in the mind of God. This calls for a conclusion outside the scope of knowledge of the witness," Monsignor Renzulli said.

"Sustained," Judge Bateman said.

Tommy thought Bateman was not giving him much leeway, but the last objection might come back to bite Monsignor Renzulli later, and he made a quick note on his legal pad.

"Ms. Batista, let's talk about your feelings—something you do know about. Do you honestly *feel* that God is calling you to be a priest?" Tommy asked.

"Yes, Mr. Riley. I truly feel that he's calling me to be a priest."

Silk had been watching the jury very carefully and noticed they were still dutifully focused on every word of Allie's testimony. Tommy had gotten everything in they had planned, and the jury was engaged. He'd shown gender discrimination, which is all he wanted to do. In the end, the verdict would come down to the justification of the defendants' actions, which was not anything Allie could testify about. Willis wrote a note to Tommy that said, "Pass."

Tommy looked at the note and then his notes and said, "Your Honor, we pass the witness."

†

Monsignor Renzulli rose from the table and calmly stepped in front of the witness stand. "Ms. Batista, if you are ordained as a Catholic priest, are you aware that you will take a vow to obey all teachings of the Catholic Church?

"Yes, Monsignor Renzulli, I'm aware of that vow."

"And are you aware that the Catholic Church teaches that only males may be validly ordained as priests?"

"Yes, Monsignor, I'm aware of that doctrine."

"Do you believe in the doctrine concerning the gender of priests?" Renzulli asked.

"No, Monsignor, I do not."

"Then how can you in good conscience take the vow to obey all teachings of the Catholic Church when you do not believe in the validity of one of the basic doctrines of the Church?" Renzulli asked.

Looking at the jury, she smiled and said, "If I'm ordained as a priest, the very fact that I'm ordained would necessarily mean that particular teaching is no longer taught by the Church. After all, I would be both a woman and an ordained priest. So I could readily take the vow to obey all doctrines then validly taught by the Church."

She noticed some of the jurors smiled back at her after her answer. Renzulli changed subjects and asked, "Ms. Batista, there has been a good bit of notoriety about your lawsuit, wouldn't you agree?"

"Yes, Monsignor."

"It might make one wonder how sincere you are about your vocation or whether you're seeking publicity."

"Objection." Tommy stood up. "Counsel is not asking a question of the witness but is lecturing her."

"Sustained. Please confine your examinations to questions, Monsignor."

Renzulli continued, "You testified that you have had the calling to be a priest since you were a child, and you feel this is a calling from God. Correct?"

"Yes."

"When did you apply to the seminary?" he asked.

"I applied about a year ago," she replied.

"Ms. Batista, you testified you are thirty-three years of age. Ninety-nine percent of all priests apply to the seminary in their twenties. Why did it take so long for you to apply to the seminary if you really believe that God called you to become a priest?" Renzulli asked.

"I don't know. You'll have to ask God." There was more laughter in the courtroom. Bateman considered using his gavel to calm the room but thought better of it.

Renzulli continued, "Unfortunately, God is not on the witness stand, Ms. Batista. You are. Again, why did it take you so long to apply to the seminary?"

"I knew that I would not be accepted. I felt that I had no recourse. But the more I prayed on it, the more I was convinced He was directing me to apply to the seminary."

Monsignor Renzulli looked at her closely and asked, "Are you aware there are many Christian religions that would readily take someone who is as dedicated as you say you are to be a priest or a minister?"

"Yes, Monsignor, I'm aware of that."

"Then why did you not apply to one of those religious seminaries, instead of filing a lawsuit against the Catholic Church to allow you entrance into the Catholic seminary?" Monsignor Renzulli asked.

"Because I'm a Catholic. I believe as others do, and as you most certainly do, that the Catholic Church was established on earth as the one true Church of our Lord and Savior. I wish to become a Catholic priest."

Monsignor Renzulli thought he saw a small opening that he wished to explore. "Ms. Batista, I have one final question. What does the word Christian mean to you?"

Allie was puzzled for a moment. She had discussed the most complicated aspects of Catholic theology with her legal team, but never something so simple.

"A Christian is anyone who follows the teachings of Christ. I—"

But Renzulli cut her off swiftly with a raised hand and a booming "Thank you, Ms. Batista." He looked at his notes and said, "No further questions, Your Honor." He smirked at Tommy as he sat.

"Any redirect examination, Mr. Riley?" Judge Bateman inquired.

Tommy realized that Renzulli had made some sort of point—he just wasn't sure what it was. "No, Your Honor."

"The witness is excused. Call your next witness, Mr. Riley," Judge Bateman said.

"The plaintiff calls Dr. Sylvia Turner," Tommy stated.

†

Dr. Turner was an attractive, middle-aged woman with gray hair. She was small with a slight build. Her horn-rimmed glasses, black suit, and white blouse made her look exactly like what she was: a college professor. Tommy spent fifteen minutes inquiring about her education, positions held, and honors received—all of which were extensive. He concluded by requesting the court to acknowledge Dr. Turner as an expert in determining the qualifications of a candidate for the seminary. Monsignor Renzulli had no objection, since Dr. Turner consulted for the archdiocese in her area of expertise. Judge Bateman certified Dr. Turner as an expert.

"Dr. Turner, will you please describe the process by which you examine potential applicants to the seminary?" Tommy asked.

"Yes, Mr. Riley," she answered. "To begin with, by the time we interview them, the candidates have been recommended by the priests and the pastor of the parish in which they live. Since priests know what it takes to be a priest, they are best able to assess whether a candidate has all the outward attributes to be a priest. The psychological evaluation amounts to culling. We're looking for two qualities that may not be readily noticeable—the absence of pathology and the presence of good mental health. We try to do this in two ways: a face-to-face interview and written examinations."

"Let's talk about the interview first. What questions do you ask?" Tommy queried.

Dr. Turner looked at the jury and said, "We ask about past sexual experiences such as, 'When was the last time you had sex?' Three years or more is the preferred answer. 'Last week' or 'this morning' would be detrimental to the candidate. In addition, we ask about masturbation fantasies, as well as romantic relationships and the cause of those breakups. We also ask about parental relationships, and alcohol and drug consumption. Depending upon the answers to all of those questions, we might go deeper—particularly in the area of alcohol and sex. We might ask how they control their sexual desires. Our observations are as important as their responses. We look to see if there is eye avoidance or other facial expressions that might indicate lying."

"Do you use a lie detector in your face-to-face interviews?" Tommy asked.

"The effectiveness of polygraphs is debatable; we rely on our training."

"Very well. Please tell us about the other examinations," Tommy said.

Again, looking at the jury she said, "All candidates must take an HIV test, which is not administered by us, and a number of written examinations, which are. An example is the Minnesota Multiphasic Personality Inventory, which screens for several things including gender confusion, paranoia, and depression. These are very detailed examinations that reveal a lot about the candidate."

"Dr. Turner, did you perform the same tests on Alejandra Batista that you use on all applicants to the seminary for the Roman Catholic Archdiocese of New Orleans?" Tommy asked, also looking at the jurors.

"Yes, I did," she said firmly.

"Based upon your interview and written examination of

Alejandra Batista, did you form an opinion about her fitness to be a candidate for the seminary?" Tommy asked.

"Yes, I did."

"What is that opinion, Dr. Turner?" Tommy asked.

"She tested admirably," Dr. Turner said forcefully. "If she had been of the right gender, there is no doubt in my mind she would have been readily accepted to the seminary."

"No further questions, Your Honor. I pass the witness," Tommy said.

Monsignor Renzulli stood up and asked, "Dr. Turner, there seems to be a lot of subjectivity rather than objectivity in your process. Would you agree with that statement?"

"Yes, Monsignor, it's not a black-and-white process. It's hard to define what we do, but it's kind of like an 'I'll know it when I see it' type of procedure," she answered directly. "Clearly if the process were objective, our expertise would be less useful."

"What is your opinion of whether a woman should be a priest?" Renzulli asked.

"I do not have one," she replied firmly.

"Really. None at all. As a woman, you have no opinion on the matter?" Renzulli countered.

"No. None at all," she answered.

"I find that difficult to believe," he replied.

"Objection," Tommy didn't even need to leave his chair for this one.

"Sustained," Judge Bateman drawled. "Monsignor Renzulli, the witness has answered the question twice. Whether or not you believe her is immaterial."

"Yes, Your Honor. Dr. Turner, are you Catholic?"

"Yes, I am."

"In your work, have you come across any studies that

show only a very small percentage of practicing Catholics don't have an opinion on this issue?"

"No, I have not."

"So you would not be able to dispute studies which show that most Catholic women have very strong opinions about whether women should or should not be allowed to the priesthood."

"No."

Renzulli looked at her and smiled; he couldn't help himself. "But you are one of the few women who don't care one way or the other?" He caught himself. "Withdrawn."

But he had engaged Dr. Turner. "Monsignor Renzulli, there is a whole world of people who try not to judge others as male or female, black or white. We invite you to join us whenever you're ready."

Renzulli looked to the Judge for help, "Your Honor, move to have that stricken from the record."

Judge Bateman stared at Renzulli, "Motion denied. To the degree that we can consider discrimination a bad thing on its face, there is nothing inherently wrong with her statement. And quite frankly, you deserved it."

"Yes, Your Honor." He turned again to Dr. Turner. "Surely in your work you have witnessed women who have been discriminated in society. Is that true?" Renzulli asked.

"Yes."

"Is the field in which you work dominated by men?"

"Mostly, but it is getting better."

"As a woman who has succeeded in a field dominated by men, is there any part of you that wants the plaintiff to succeed in her quest to be a priest that might have influenced the subjective part of your process?" asked Renzulli, somewhat heatedly.

Dr. Turner matched the tone that was in Renzulli's voice. "Monsignor, the reason I have succeeded in a field dominated by men is that I am not biased by gender or anything else. I have done one thing and one thing only. I call 'em like I see 'em."

Monsignor Renzulli once again looked at his notes and said, "No further questions, Your Honor."

"Mr. Riley, do you have any redirect?"

"No, Your Honor," Tommy answered.

Judge Bateman looked at the clock and announced, "We're coming up on the lunch hour. These proceedings will be adjourned until two o'clock. Court is dismissed until that time."

CHAPTER THIRTY-FIVE

After lunch, Monsignor Renzulli called Archbishop Sierra to the stand. *Now the real action begins*, Tommy thought. Everything up to now had been about establishing the record for what everyone knew: the only reason Alejandra Batista was not accepted to the seminary was because of her gender. He was confident that Renzulli hadn't successfully impeached Dr. Turner's objectivity on her other qualifications. Other than gender, he had proven Allie was an excellent candidate. Now it was time to see if the Church could justify its actions.

After peremptory questions by Monsignor Renzulli about the Archbishop's education, training, and positions held in the Church—all of which duly impressed the room—Renzulli began to get to the heart of the testimony.

"You are the head of the Archdiocese of New Orleans. Is that correct?" Monsignor Renzulli asked.

"Yes, that is correct," Archbishop Sierra answered quietly.

"As bishop of a diocese, are you a cardinal of the Catholic Church?" Renzulli asked.

"Yes, I am," Archbishop Sierra answered again.

"Is that the highest designation in the Catholic Church, other than his Holy Father, the Pope?" Renzulli inquired.

"Yes, it is," Sierra answered humbly.

"Is that why you may be called either Archbishop Sierra or Bishop Cardinal Sierra?" Monsignor Renzulli asked.

"Yes," Sierra responded.

"Which title do you prefer?"

"Just 'bishop' is fine with me," Sierra said, smiling at the jury as they smiled back.

"As head of the Catholic Church in New Orleans, are you the ultimate authority to approve or disapprove an applicant to the seminary in this archdiocese?" Monsignor Renzulli asked.

"Yes, I am."

"What are the basic qualifications for an applicant to be admitted to the seminary?"

Archbishop Sierra responded, "The basic qualifications are that the candidate must be an unmarried male baptized and confirmed in the Roman Catholic Church."

"Why are unmarried women baptized and confirmed in the Roman Catholic Church not qualified?" Renzulli asked.

"It has been the teaching of the Catholic Church since the time of Christ that all priests shall be of the male gender," Archbishop Sierra answered forcefully.

"Is there a direct scriptural reference that is the foundation for this teaching?" Monsignor Renzulli asked.

"No, there is not."

"Then, Archbishop Sierra, will you please explain to the jury the foundation of this doctrine?" Monsignor Renzulli asked.

"Yes, I will be glad to."

Archbishop Sierra then turned and looked directly at the jury and said, "Let's begin with His Last Supper. Twelve apostles were ordained by Jesus as the first priests of the Catholic Church. Jesus had many women among His followers and could have easily chosen a woman to be among these apostles, but He did not. The fact that He did not appoint a woman is very significant. We follow the example that Jesus set two thousand years ago."

"Bishop Sierra, what were the social conditions of a woman in Palestine and Jerusalem at the time of Jesus?" Renzulli asked.

"The society in which Jesus lived was very much a male-dominated society. Women were considered little more than slaves. There was no equality at all among men and women at the time," Archbishop Sierra answered.

"Perhaps the fact that Jesus did not appoint a woman as an apostle was because He was following the social norms of the times. No?" Monsignor Renzulli asked.

"No."

"Why is that not true, Bishop Sierra?" Renzulli asked.

Again looking at the jury, Archbishop Sierra said, "Unlike the males of His time, Jesus treated women equally in all respects, which was a total break from the social customs of the times. He was establishing a new religion—one that caused much controversy and was very different from the Hebrew religion, which had only male rabbis. At the time, there were many non-Hebrew religions that had women as priestesses. He could easily have named a woman as an apostle, and it wouldn't have been extraordinary for His new religion. It would also have been accepted by the disciples. The fact that He did not do so is proof that He did not wish to do so."

"For what other reasons does the Church offer the priesthood exclusively to men?"

Archbishop Sierra responded, again speaking directly to the jury. "Jesus Christ's example for selecting only men to the priesthood has been followed ever since His death and resurrection.

The apostles, who knew Jesus better than anyone besides His mother, had an opportunity to name a woman to replace Judas. Judas was one of the original apostles who betrayed Jesus Christ and later committed suicide. The Bible mentions many women who were followers of Jesus and who would have been excellent candidates to be named as an apostle and therefore a priest.

"One of those women was His mother, Mary, whom the early church venerated as the mother of God and still does so today. The apostles knew her well; more importantly, they knew the love for her that Jesus had. She would have been the perfect replacement. Remember, Mary was very young when she conceived. She was likely still only in her 40s when He died. She would have been a great choice. Yet they did not choose the perfect person to replace Judas. There is no evidence that anyone thought otherwise, or that she wished to be appointed. She knew Jesus better than anybody, which suggests she knew that her appointment as an apostle was not His will. After all, Jesus could have appointed her in the first place and did not. The will of Jesus Christ has been faithfully followed by the Catholic Church ever since."

Renzulli looked at the jury and saw they were held in rapt attention. He glanced back at Sierra and said, "Are there more reasons, other than what you have provided so far?"

"There are," Archbishop Sierra replied. "Jesus was also God, and He could have easily been born a woman but He chose to be a man. He constantly referred to His Father, who had also chosen to be recognized as the Father of the Hebrew religion in the Old Testament. But Jesus Christ as God became man, which Catholics call the incarnation. God became a man, not a woman—He took a very specific form of gender. With all due respect to the estimable Dr. Turner—and

I so enjoyed her testimony—" Archbishop Sierra's eyes briefly alighted on Tommy before returning to the jury, "gender is still a real thing, and gender still matters in many aspects of life."

"Can you give us an example?" Renzulli intoned smugly.

"I can. Priests are the representatives of Christ. More than that, they are the embodiment of Jesus, from the word body. Literally the form of the human being He took on earth. A woman cannot properly embody Christ on earth because Jesus was a man; therefore, priests are also men. Women are exalted in the Catholic religion. It is not for any discriminatory reason that they cannot join the priesthood. It is the way that we choose to worship."

He said it so simply and with such conviction that Tommy wondered briefly if he was the sincerest believer—or the greatest actor on the planet.

Monsignor Renzulli lifted his notes, folded them, and said, "Thank you, Archbishop Sierra, I have no further questions."

Monsignor Renzulli and Archbishop Sierra had talked at length about his testimony and strategy. They had agreed that Archbishop Sierra would state the Church's position and the reasoning behind it and leave it at that. They had established a quite justifiable and defensible reason for the Church's position. Riley had no witnesses to refute Archbishop Sierra's testimony, and it would be up to Riley to try to punch holes in it on cross-examination. As he sat down, Monsignor Renzulli said a silent prayer that he had not underestimated Riley.

"Your witness, Mr. Riley," Judge Bateman said.

CHAPTER THIRTY-SIX

"Bishop Sierra," Tommy began, "I believe you said there is no direct scriptural revelation that Jesus of Nazareth wanted to forever bar women from the priesthood and to reserve that honor to males only into perpetuity. Is that correct?"

"There is no direct order by Jesus in the scriptures to reserve the priesthood for males only," Sierra answered.

"So your answer would be yes, correct?" Tommy said firmly.

"In the context in which I have just stated it, my answer is yes," Sierra responded firmly.

Tommy continued, "Without an explicit direction in the scriptures, I believe your testimony is that the Church relies upon what Jesus Christ didn't do but could have done in appointing males only as the twelve apostles. Is that correct?" Tommy asked.

"Yes, that is correct," Sierra answered.

"Why did Jesus appoint twelve apostles instead of two, ten, or twenty?" Tommy asked.

"The twelve apostles corresponded to the twelve tribes of Israel, which was in fulfillment of the Hebrew scriptures," Archbishop Sierra answered.

"Were any of the twelve tribes of Israel led by a woman at that time or before that time?" Tommy asked.

"Not that we are aware of," Archbishop Sierra responded.

"So it would have made sense at the time to continue the tradition to have all males as the twelve apostles. Is that correct?" Tommy asked.

"I don't understand your question," Sierra said.

"I'll put it another way. The number of apostles was selected intentionally to match the number of the tribes of Israel. Is that right?" Tommy asked.

"Yes, that's what we understand."

"If Jesus, as you surmise, was following the tradition of the tribes of Israel, which had an all-male hierarchy, wouldn't it have made sense to continue the all-male hierarchy in the appointment of apostles?" Tommy asked again.

"Possibly," Sierra answered.

"He was starting a new religion different from, but in fulfillment of, the Hebrew religion, correct?"

"Yes."

"Wouldn't His new religion eventually have to break from the traditions of the Hebrew religion? Otherwise it would be the same religion, not a totally new one. Correct?" Tommy asked.

"It's actually the opposite. His religion, as you call it, was so different from the previous tradition that He was put to death for it. It was more a question of respecting the Hebrew tradition sufficiently so that He could acquire followers as His teachings veered away from the old ways. Improved them, we would say."

"Fair enough. Good point." Tommy continued, "As His new religion developed and broke away from the traditions of the Hebrew religion, what made sense to do at the start would no longer be required many, many years later. Is that correct?"

"I suppose so. There are essential and non-essential elements in any society of human beings. If the tradition or practice was also a fundamental part of the new religion, it would still be required in perpetuity. This is the reasoning for the male-only priesthood, in case you were coming to that," Sierra said calmly.

He had the same serene expression in his eyes, but with an added twinkle that let Tommy know he was enjoying the verbal jousting every bit as much as the two lawyers. Tommy stared back with a smile.

"Are you aware that, aside from the Orthodox sect, Judaism now ordains women as Rabbis?" Tommy asked.

"My focus in life is on the Catholic religion, Mr. Riley, not on the Jewish religion. I don't see how their rules of ordination would have any bearing on what we do," Sierra said politely.

"Great. Then let's talk about some of the other characteristics the original apostles had besides being male," Tommy said. "Would you agree that they all probably wore beards, since that was one of the social norms of the time?"

"Yes."

"Did Jesus mean to forever exclude priests who were clean shaven?" Tommy asked.

"No, of course not. That was an incidental characteristic that the apostles shared at the time," Archbishop Sierra answered.

"Yes, Bishop Sierra, that would be ridiculous, wouldn't it? He probably would not even have had a choice to select someone who was clean shaven anyway, would he?" Tommy asked.

"Highly unlikely," Sierra answered. "The early Church was not a clean-shaven group as a rule."

"As the social customs changed and beards were no longer in fashion, that characteristic would not be relevant at all, would it?" Tommy asked.

"It wasn't relevant in the first place. Beards were merely coincidental characteristics."

"I believe you also said that it was a social custom at the time not to put women in a position of leadership since they were treated only slightly above slaves. Is that correct?" Tommy asked.

Archbishop Sierra adjusted himself in the witness chair and said, "Yes, I said that."

"The custom of treating women as little more than slaves has also changed over time. Correct?" Tommy asked.

"It most certainly has," Sierra answered.

"In summary, we have two social customs at the time of Jesus that defined the apostles, both of which have changed over time. One you and the Catholic Church deem relevant. The other you deem irrelevant to the qualifications of a priest today. Is that correct?" Tommy asked.

"Yes, a beard is merely incidental. Gender is fundamental," Archbishop Sierra responded firmly.

"So you say," Tommy said. "Now let's talk about a few final characteristics of the apostles. Most theologians believe all the apostles were probably married. If indeed that was the case, did that mean Jesus intended priests to be married in the future?" Tommy asked.

"No."

"If He intended it, that would fly directly in the face of the doctrine of the Catholic Church requiring priests to be exactly the opposite, which is unmarried. Wouldn't it?" Tommy asked.

"Yes," Sierra responded.

"So the fact that they were married was merely incidental and not fundamental?" Tommy asked.

Archbishop Sierra sighed and said, "Yes, if in fact they were all married."

"All of the first apostles were also Jews, weren't they?" Tommy asked.

"Yes."

"There were a number of non-Jews, or what were called Gentiles at the time, among His followers. Is that true?" Tommy asked.

"Yes."

"Then He certainly could have appointed one or more Gentiles to be among the original apostles, is that correct?"

"Yes, He could have," Archbishop Sierra answered.

"Does the fact that He didn't appoint Gentiles to be among the original apostles mean that Gentiles were barred forever from the priesthood?" Tommy inquired.

"No."

Tommy looked directly at the jury and asked Sierra, "Why not, Bishop Sierra?"

Archbishop Sierra responded, "The original church was comprised mostly of Jews. As that church followed His command to 'go and teach all nations,' Gentiles became an integral part of the Church, and it was natural that Gentile men would become ordained as priests."

"Since the original church was comprised mostly of Jewish people, it would have been very difficult to appoint a Gentile into a religious hierarchy like the Twelve Apostles. Is that not correct?" Tommy asked.

"Objection. Question calls for a conclusion of the witness," Monsignor Renzulli exclaimed.

"Your Honor," Tommy said, "the witness is an archbishop

and cardinal in the Roman Catholic Church. It is the second highest office in the Church. Certainly his scope of knowledge would include the reasons for the actions of Jesus Christ. He has already given an opinion in direct testimony about some of his own activities."

After a moment of thought, Judge Bateman said, "Objection is overruled. Please answer the question, Bishop Sierra."

"Jesus could have done whatever He wanted and appointed whomever He wanted to be one of His apostles," Sierra said firmly.

"Yes, indeed. You have said that. He could have appointed a woman or a Gentile to be an apostle, despite the tremendous social pressures that existed, but He didn't. Yet His example concerning the exclusion of Gentiles and women as one of the original priests is followed today by your church *only* with respect to women, correct?"

Archbishop Sierra looked at Tommy and said, "Yes."

Tommy looked at his notes, at the jury, then directly at Archbishop Sierra and said, "Bishop Sierra, I would like to summarize your testimony and make sure the jury and I understand it. Jesus appointed twelve apostles. They all had common characteristics, such as a beard, marriage status, common language, and little or no education. As the Church grew and social customs and mores changed, the Church determined that those characteristics were merely incidental for the priesthood. However, their gender was fundamental. Why was the gender of the original apostles the only fundamental characteristic, while all the rest of the characteristics of the apostles were incidental? Aren't they all the result of the social customs of the times in which Jesus lived?"

"For the reasons I previously stated," Archbishop Sierra answered.

"Do you not see the inconsistency in your testimony?" Tommy asked pointedly.

Archbishop Sierra looked directly back at Tommy and said, "No, I don't. Not at all."

"Let's talk some more about what you have previously testified. You stated that women were little more than slaves but that Jesus treated women equally with men. Is that correct?"

"Yes."

"Now, was slavery an accepted social custom of the times in which Jesus lived?" Tommy asked.

"Yes. It was readily accepted in Roman society."

"Could Jesus have appointed a slave as an apostle?" Tommy asked.

"I have said, He could have chosen anyone," Archbishop Sierra answered.

"But He didn't appoint a slave, did he?" Tommy continued.

"No, He didn't."

"No, He didn't. In fact, he often used the relationship of master and slave in His parables to His disciples, didn't he?" Tommy asked.

"Yes."

"But He never spoke out against slavery in His parables or in His teachings, did he?" Tommy asked.

"Not that I am aware of," Archbishop Sierra answered.

"Why do you suppose He didn't take a stand against slavery and speak out against it, as He did of many other practices that He disagreed with at the time?" Tommy asked.

"I don't know," Archbishop Sierra answered.

"Could it be that slavery was so ingrained in the social norms of the time that if He had done so it would have been on the order of a tremendous social reform? Could it be that the times were not right for such a revolutionary idea and to do so would take the focus away from the religious reform He was trying to establish?" Tommy asked.

Archbishop Sierra raised his eyebrows and said, "As I have said, I don't know His reasons for not choosing slaves to be apostles. And I would not presume to know."

"I only asked you if it was possible," Tommy responded.

"Anything is possible, but not everything is probable," Archbishop Sierra pointedly replied.

"Was Jesus put on earth to undertake a revolution of social upheaval?" Tommy asked.

Archbishop Sierra took a moment and clasped his hands in front of him. "Your question is far more complicated perhaps than you intend. But the short answer is no."

"What about putting a woman in a position of leadership? Would the male-dominated society in which Jesus lived have rebelled against such a revolutionary social change so that the message He was trying to deliver about religious reform might have lost focus? Is that also possible?" Tommy asked.

"Mr. Riley, I see where you're going and, yes, anything is possible. But again—"

"The truth is, He didn't seek to abolish the entrenched custom of slavery and He didn't seek to abolish the entrenched custom of male-only leadership, correct?" Tommy asked.

"That's correct. He didn't seek to abolish it at the time. One could argue, as you seem inclined to, that through His teachings He put mechanisms in place that would eventually tear down injustices of all kinds. Though certainly some injustices persisted for centuries, as do many to this present day."

"Such as women being excluded from the priesthood?"

"Objection. Counsel is badgering His Eminence," Renzulli said.

After a moment, Judge Bateman said, "The objection is sustained. Try to stay on track, Mr. Riley."

"Yes, Your Honor. Now, Bishop Sierra, I believe you testified that the original apostles became ordained as priests at the Last Supper. Is that correct?"

"Yes."

"Would women have also been present at the Last Supper?"

"That's a good question. I don't know," Archbishop Sierra responded.

Tommy looked at Archbishop Sierra with a puzzled look on his face and said, "I believe you said that Jesus treated women equally with men and that they were included as part of His disciples. Is that true?"

"Yes, I said that."

"Would the apostles have cooked the meal, or would women have prepared it in the time of Jesus?" Tommy asked.

"Women, most certainly," Sierra answered.

"Would Jesus have thrown the women out of the meal after they had prepared it, or would He have treated them equally with the men, as you have said was His custom?" Tommy asked.

"I don't know," Archbishop Sierra responded. "It's a very interesting question but my knowledge of the Bible is as it relates to the dogma of the Church, not the social mores of the time."

"Your knowledge seems to be driven by convenience depending on the question, Bishop Sierra," Tommy said sarcastically.

Monsignor Renzulli stood quickly, "Objection."

"Sustained. The jury will ignore that last comment by Mr. Riley," Judge Bateman said. "You may continue."

Tommy turned to Archbishop Sierra and said, "Bishop Sierra, let's assume Jesus followed His usual custom—there is ample scriptural evidence—and women were present at the meal. Would Jesus have been speaking to them as well when He said, 'Do this in remembrance of me'?"

"No."

"It is not possible?" Tommy asked

Archbishop Sierra said sternly, "No, it's not possible."

Tommy replied quickly, "You said anything was possible."

Archbishop Sierra glared at Tommy, dropping his mask for the first time. "Yes, Mr. Riley. Anything, except that."

CHAPTER THIRTY-SEVEN

After a short recess, Tommy Riley continued his cross-examination of Archbishop Sierra.

"Bishop Sierra, what do the scriptures and the Catholic Church say happened on the feast of Pentecost?"

Archbishop Sierra answered, "Jesus had risen from the dead, and all the disciples were gathered in a locked upper room, where they stayed when they were in Jerusalem, because they were afraid of reprisals from the Jews. Jesus walked through the walls and the locked doors and breathed the Holy Spirit upon them."

After several moments of silence, Tommy asked, "Is that all that happened?"

"I don't know what you mean by your question," Archbishop Sierra responded.

"Did Jesus not also say, 'Whose sins you shall forgive, they are forgiven them; and whose sins you shall retain, they are retained,' to all those in the room?"

"Yes, He did."

"Are those words the foundation for the Sacrament of Penance for the Catholic Church?"

"It is one of the foundations," Sierra answered.

"Are priests the only ones who can administer the Sacrament of Penance or Reconciliation?"

"Yes."

"And the power to administer the Sacrament of Penance, in which the penitent is forgiven his or her sins, was given to those in the room that day and has since been passed on to their successors, correct?" Tommy asked.

Archbishop Sierra stirred in his chair, looked at Monsignor Renzulli, who stared right back at him, both wondering where Tommy was going with this, and finally answered, "Yes."

"At the time of the Pentecost, were the disciples following the example of Jesus and treating women equally? Or had they reverted to their old ways of excluding them? In other words, were women present when Christ conferred the powers of the Sacrament of Penance?" Tommy asked.

Archbishop Sierra knew Tommy had boxed him in. If women were present, they could arguably have received priestly orders for the Sacrament of Penance as well as the men. If women were not there, the apostles had reverted to their social customs of excluding women, which could account for the early church not appointing women to be priests.

"The scriptures do not say specifically one way or the other," Archbishop Sierra said.

"So, women might have been there, correct?"

"Yes."

"When Jesus conferred the priestly orders of the Sacrament of Penance on all the people in the room, if women had been there they would have received those orders as well, correct?"

"No."

"Why not? Did He say, 'Whose sins you *men* shall forgive,' or did He say, 'Whose sins you shall forgive'?"

"Mr. Riley, you're taking scripture out of context," Archbishop Sierra said passionately. "As I have said, when the scriptures are understood in their entirety it is clear the intent of Jesus was to restrict the priesthood to men. You cannot just single out phrases; you must consider the big picture."

"Yes, Bishop Sierra, that's indeed what you have said," Tommy said, looking at the jury with a bemused look. "Now, please answer my question and tell us what the Catholic scriptures say Jesus said. 'Whose sins you men shall forgive,' or, 'Whose sins you shall forgive'?"

"The second one," Sierra responded.

"Now let's go to another dogma of the Church. Would you explain to the jury what church dogma is?" Tommy said.

Looking at the jury, Sierra said, "Happily. Dogma is a fundamental belief of the Church. Dogma is an infallible teaching that cannot be ignored."

"Is it a dogma of the Catholic Church that men and women are equal in the eyes of God?"

"Yes, certainly."

"Bishop Sierra, on the one hand you have a fundamental belief that men and women are equal in the eyes of God. But to be a representative of Jesus on earth, women are not equal to men and do not have the honor to serve as a representative of Jesus."

"It isn't about honor, Mr. Riley."

"It isn't an honor?"

Archbishop Sierra looked at Tommy with a patronizing smile and briefly touched his mouth to keep from laughing.

"Please answer the question, Bishop Sierra," said Judge Bateman.

"Yes. Certainly. I apologize for laughing but I see now perhaps why you have difficulty understanding. Of course, it's an honor in the sense that the priesthood is a position of respect. But we do not honor ourselves, Mr. Riley. All of the honor is directed to our Lord and Savior Jesus Christ. Man—and woman—honor themselves only to the extent that they honor our Lord. Surely you are familiar with transubstantiation?"

Tommy smiled back, "With respect, I'll ask the questions Bishop Sierra. Do you wish to point out that during the Eucharist the bread and wine become the body and blood of Christ?"

Archbishop Sierra nodded. "You understand it then."

"So you're referring to your previous use of the word embodiment?"

"I see you do understand. Forgive me. I was mistaken."

Tommy turned to face the jury. "Bishop Sierra, you said earlier that priests were men because they embody Christ, and Jesus was a man?"

"It's really quite simple."

Tommy stared hard at each of the jurors. Then he turned. "Yes, Bishop Sierra, it's extremely simple. Why couldn't a woman embody a man? For that matter, why can't a man embody a woman? We are all flesh and blood, we are all human. Created equal in the eyes of God, an infallible doctrine?"

Archbishop Sierra turned red. "Because it's preposterous."

"You don't see the conflict between these two 'infallible' truths of the Church?"

"No, I do not," Archbishop Sierra said firmly.

Tommy responded heatedly, "One is based upon the teachings and examples of Jesus, and the other is based upon what He *didn't* say and *didn't* do? You don't see a conflict?"

"No, I do not," Sierra replied resolutely.

Tommy looked at the jury and rolled his eyes and looked back to Archbishop Sierra and said, "One last question, Bishop Sierra. You've been here during the entire trial, have you not?"

"You know that I have, yes."

"Do you remember when Monsignor Renzulli objected to the question I asked Ms. Batista about whether she knew if God wanted her to be a priest?"

"Yes."

"Do you remember that Monsignor Renzulli said that Ms. Batista could not possibly know what was in the mind of God and that was outside her scope of knowledge?" Tommy asked.

"Yes," Archbishop Sierra answered.

"Now I ask you, without any scriptural evidence, how can you and the other men of the Catholic Church possibly know what's in the mind of God concerning the gender of His priests?"

Archbishop Sierra took a moment and said, "The Catholic Church is the embodiment of the Word and will of God on earth. When Jesus made Peter His first Pope, the scriptures are clear that Peter maintained his power on earth, and that all of the popes, including the present one, are in direct succession to Peter. When popes speak on matters of faith and morals, they are infallible in that pronouncement. They cannot do otherwise. They are guided by God in the form of the Holy Spirit, and what they say is the will of God. The pope has declared that the priesthood should be limited to the male gender, based upon the clear example of Jesus. And that, Mr. Riley, is the will of God."

"Thank you, Bishop Sierra. I have no further questions."

†

"Do you have any questions on redirect, Monsignor Renzulli?" Judge Bateman asked.

"Yes, I do, Your Honor."

"Then you may proceed."

"Bishop Sierra," Monsignor Riley began. "Mr. Riley asked you about the equality of women within the Church. Does the Church consider women inferior to men?" Monsignor Renzulli asked.

"Certainly not. Women are not denied the priesthood by the designs of men, but rather because it is the plan of *God*. Women can do things that men cannot do such as give life. Men can never do that. The church has been overtly clear in many areas and in many things about the absolute equality of men and women. It's simply a historical fact and an unbroken tradition that women cannot be priests any more than men can bear human life. Jesus likens himself as the bridegroom and the Church as the bride. Men have the means and protective aspects of a bridegroom, and a woman doesn't have those any more than a man has the instincts of a woman in giving birth and nurturing life," Archbishop Sierra responded.

"Mr. Riley has tried to make a point that the social customs of the day would have prevented Jesus Christ from appointing a woman to be an apostle. Do you agree with that statement?"

"No, I do not."

"Why do you not agree?"

"If one is a Christian, then one has to believe that Jesus Christ was God incarnate into man. If one is not a Christian, then what He did or did not do is of no relevance. As God, He could have chosen anyone He wanted to be an apostle, regardless of social restrictions, and His truth would have prevailed. His Word was truth. The fact He only named men as His apostles is part of His Word and is what the Church has believed and taught for over two thousand years. All the other characteristics I was asked about were merely incidental and irrelevant. A woman cannot and will never be a priest," Archbishop Sierra answered.

"The plaintiff and her counsel have mentioned having the proper genitalia to be a priest. Is genitalia relevant to the priesthood?"

"No, it is not."

"Will you please explain your answer?"

"Gladly. The presence of male genitalia is only one of many characteristics of a man. Men and women have a totally different biology because of gender. Gender is fundamental to a human being. As an example, the brains of the two genders are different, both chemically and structurally, leading to different programming. Whatever the current cultural climate asserts on the matter of gender identity, it is the firm stance of the Church that a woman, no matter how many surgeries she has, is still a woman. And a man, no matter how many surgeries he has, is still a man."

Monsignor Renzulli looked at the jury for a moment; being satisfied with what he saw, he said, "No further questions, Your Honor."

†

"Do you have any further cross examination, Mr. Riley?" Judge Bateman asked.

"Yes, Your Honor, I do," Tommy said. "Bishop Sierra, you have testified that the basic qualifications for an applicant to the seminary and the priesthood are an unmarried male baptized and confirmed in the Catholic Church. Is that correct?"

"Yes."

"It has come to my attention that you have ordained married males. Is that correct?" Tommy asked cryptically.

Archbishop Sierra looked puzzled at first, then appeared to recognize where Tommy was going. But he still needed time to formulate an answer. "I'm not sure what you mean. Perhaps you can jog my memory."

"I will be glad to, Bishop Sierra. Have you not ordained a married Episcopal priest into the priesthood of the Catholic Church?"

"Yes."

"Would you explain to the jury how this is possible given the basic qualifications you just told the jury?"

"The Episcopalian religion is quite similar in all respects to the Catholic religion, except for their allegiance to the pope. The pope has given special dispensation to ordain married Episcopal priests when circumstances warrant, including a vow of papal allegiance," Archbishop Sierra answered.

"The Episcopalian religion also ordains women priests, does it not?"

"I believe it does."

"Will the Catholic Church ordain a female priest of the Episcopal religion, married or unmarried?"

"No."

"So is it your testimony that you and the Pope and the other cardinals have found a way to bend the rules to allow *married* male Episcopal priests to be ordained despite the basic qualifications. Yet you will not afford the same accommodation to a *woman* in the same circumstances?" Tommy asked incredulously.

There was a long moment of silence, and Tommy said, "Never mind, Bishop Sierra, I withdraw the question. We already know your answer." Tommy tossed a glance at the jury on his way back to the table, but then turned back.

"I have one more question, Bishop Sierra. Does the Catholic Church believe it is the Church established by Jesus Christ?"

"Yes, it does."

"Is it fair to say that the Catholic Church considers itself to be the one, true Christian church?"

"It is the only church that has not wavered from the example and teachings of Jesus Christ from then until now," Archbishop Sierra said calmly.

"No further questions, Your Honor," Tommy said.

"Monsignor Renzulli, do you have any further questions for Bishop Sierra?" Judge Bateman asked.

"No, Your Honor."

Judge Bateman continued, "We are close to five o'clock. This court will adjourn until tomorrow morning at nine o'clock when we will have closing arguments of counsel, after which time the jury will retire to deliberate in conformance with the instructions I will give to the jury."

"All rise," the bailiff said, and Judge Bateman left the bench and retired to his chambers.

†

Michel Vachon made his way through the TV reporters on the way out of the courtroom, barely able to contain his fury. The heretic lawyer had just reduced Archbishop Sierra to mincemeat. But his animus for the archbishop himself was nearly as strong as the hatred he bore for the lawyer. How could such an imbecile become archbishop and a cardinal of His Church? Michel would have answered Riley's questions infinitely better on cross-examination than the archbishop. It was clear that Monsignor Renzulli's strategy to rely on Archbishop Sierra was doomed to backfire.

He would wait for the inevitable phone call, but at this point it was a formality. God would call Michel to act, and he would be ready.

CHAPTER THIRTY-EIGHT

Tommy sat propped up in bed, going over the points he would make in his closing argument the next day, when his telephone rang.

"Hello, this is Tommy Riley," he said.

"Mr. Riley, this is Sister Agnes. I live with Alejandra Batista," the other voice said.

"Yes, Sister Agnes, I know who you are. What can I do for you?"

"Is Allie with you, Mr. Riley?" she said with alarm.

"No. Should she be?" Tommy answered.

"I don't know," she said. She sounded panicked.

"What's happened, Sister Agnes?"

"Allie received a call from a lawyer in your office, Gerald Grant. He said he was outside our house and had an important document from you to give to her. She was to read it and call you immediately afterward."

Tommy shot upright in his bed.

"Sister Agnes, we need to find Allie."

†

Five minutes later, Roy Yardley answered his house phone on the third ring. "This had better be good, Tommy," he said, reading his caller ID.

"Roy, my client, Alejandra Batista, is missing. I have very good reason to suspect she's been kidnapped."

Tommy related his conversation with Sister Agnes.

"Have you tried her family and friends? It's clearly been a stressful trial. Could she be chilling out somewhere for the night?" Yardley asked.

"Roy, I know her very well and she's not chilling out somewhere."

"I have to run all of the normal traps first, Tommy, before I can go to emergency mode. I will do the best I can in the fastest time possible; I'll call you back when I either know something or when we go to plan B. Good enough?"

"Good enough."

†

The nights when Tommy was in trial he seldom slept. This was worse than any case-related adrenaline. Every minute that passed without hearing from Allie or Roy, Tommy descended further and further into panic mode. He fired back a few shots of Black Bush to calm his nerves, but it didn't help. At 5:30 a.m., his phone rang. It was Roy.

"Tommy, we've contacted everyone we can and we can't find any trace of her. I can't meet with Chief DeFreitas for a few hours but I've already requested his consideration to initiate the Gulf Coast Task Force."

"When will you know?" Tommy asked.

"When are you due in court?" Yardley inquired.

"At 9 o'clock," Tommy responded.

"We'll be cutting it close but you'll hear from me before then." And with that, he hung up.

†

When Manuel dropped Tommy at the rear entrance of the federal building at eight thirty that morning, his cell phone rang.

"The chief has initiated the task force," Roy said. "It'll be run by the New Orleans Police Department and the man in charge is Sergeant Sam Pierce. I know Sam well. There's not a better person to lead this. We're operating under the assumption she's still in the area, but we also have the FBI looped in, just in case someone took her out of state. We'll find her, Tommy," and he hung up. Sure, they'd find her, Tommy thought—but in what shape? Who would do this?

CHAPTER THIRTY-NINE

"Who are you?" she rasped in a voice she barely recognized.

"I am the instrument of the Lamb of God," a low voice growled.

As her mind raced to approach her situation rationally, Allie summoned all her internal reserves, which she was surprised to find intact.

"And just what does that have to do with me?" she said in a bold voice, trying to sound as normal as possible.

"You are a heretic, Ms. Batista," the man said calmly. "There's only one answer for heresy: total repentance and absolution for your sins. And total remorse can be obtained only through the penance of pain."

Michel Vachon closed his eyes and took a deep breath, "You're looking at the instrument of your penance. And only when God has told me your soul has been cleansed will you exit this life—free of sin, to be reunited with the Lamb of God."

Her mind whirled as she tried to make some sense of all this. She tried to be rational, but this was not rational.

"Please," she whispered. "You don't have to do this."

"There is no choice in doing the will of God, heretic. His will be done."

And with that, he uncoiled his right hand from behind his back. Gripped tightly in his fist was a thick leather handle that sprouted frayed-leather strands. Small metal pellets strung along the straps sparkled menacingly in the diffused candlelight. As he stepped close to her, bile rose in her throat. Next came the pain, cascading through her spine and shooting through every nerve in her body.

She heard her own screams echoing from a great distance, as though she were not a part of this madness at all. And for a moment, this gave her relief. Until another shockwave of agony silenced everything. This time she felt hot tears on her cheeks. She did what she'd done countless times before. She prayed. And then, mercifully, she felt nothing.

CHAPTER FORTY

After arranging to see Judge Bateman in chambers, both teams were escorted into the judge's inner sanctum. Tommy was struck by how unassuming the man seemed not dressed in his judicial robes. Judge Bateman looked up from his desk with a pen in hand and said, "Gentlemen, what can I do for you? Have you come to advise me of a settlement? And here I was just starting to enjoy myself."

Tommy and Monsignor Renzulli sat down in warm leather chairs before Judge Bateman's desk, and Tommy began. "Nothing quite as simple as that, Your Honor." He related the events of the previous evening and the call from Roy Yardley he had received that morning.

Renzulli was clearly shocked by Allie's disappearance but immediately recognized the implications for his team and went right into defensive mode.

"Your Honor, can we be sure that Ms. Batista didn't get cold feet? Or that Mr. Riley isn't hiding her somewhere? Is this something cooked up to try to lay blame on my clients or gain the sympathy of the jury?"

Tommy Riley bristled, turning his entire body toward Renzulli. He was fuming but kept his anger in check, and pointed. "I don't know what you think of me, Monsignor, but do you honestly believe I would go so far as to fraudulently initiate a Gulf Coast Task Force just to gain an advantage in a lawsuit?"

Judge Bateman interrupted, looking grave. "To say the least, this is highly unusual. I'll ask you first, Mr. Riley, since you're counsel for the plaintiff. What do you want the court to do?"

Tommy thought a moment and answered, "At the very least, a continuance until the plaintiff has been found. A party is entitled to be in court for all proceedings, and this is no different than if she had taken ill."

Judge Bateman responded, "I disagree with you, Mr. Riley. A party is entitled to be in court for all testimony so they can assist counsel with direct and cross-examination of other witnesses. I'm not aware of any rule that requires a party to be present for closing arguments and/or for the rendering of verdict. After the conclusion of testimony, they become bystanders like anyone else—just with more on the line."

"I would like time to research that point and file a brief, Your Honor," Tommy said.

Judge Bateman growled, "We don't have the time, counselor. I have indulged myself with your very interesting religious and philosophical banter, but I must keep my docket moving. Alleged criminals await. Request denied. Monsignor Renzulli, what are your thoughts?"

"Your Honor, any stay in the proceedings because of unknown reasons for the plaintiff's disappearance will undoubtedly be prejudicial to my clients. Doubtless there will be those who will think my clients had something to do with her disappearance, to prevent her from continuing her pursuit to become a seminarian and ultimately a priest. While nothing could be farther from the truth, the inference could be made and that could be highly prejudicial."

Judge Bateman thought a moment and then said, "Yes, Monsignor, I see your point, and it's a good one. Mr. Riley, what is your response?"

Tommy decided to ad lib. "It's quite common for the task force to find someone within twenty-four hours." Tommy hoped that was true. "Give me that, at least."

Judge Bateman looked at them both and said, "We must also consider a worst-case scenario."

Tommy looked at Monsignor Renzulli, who was equally confused.

"I do not mean to be glib, only pragmatic. But if indeed Ms. Batista was abducted, the person or persons who abducted her obviously do not have her best interests at heart," Judge Bateman said. "If the police find her in the next twenty-four hours, she is as likely to be dead as alive. That's the only way the perpetrator can absolutely ensure that she does not attain her goal of becoming a priest. Correct?"

Tommy felt an inward shudder, but both he and Monsignor Renzulli continued to look at Judge Bateman—curious where he was going with this.

Judge Bateman continued, "If she is found dead within the next twenty-four hours, we will not need to continue with these proceedings. Although a horrible and tragic outcome, as a practical matter she would have no legal right to pursue her quest to attend the seminary. If she's found alive within the next twenty-four hours, then we can proceed as planned. If her situation is unknown at this time tomorrow, we could still proceed to the jury without her. I believe that's the best solution for all concerned, to stay the proceedings for the next twenty-four hours."

The Judge seemed to be stating the obvious but Tommy was just relieved to get the delay.

Then Renzulli asked, "What about possible prejudice to my clients, Your Honor? In either event?"

"I will instruct them that they are to consider the evidence without regard to the plaintiff's absence being caused by the influence of you, your clients, or Mr. Riley. If the jury finds for the plaintiff, then I can postpone my decision on the mandatory injunction until she reappears. If she's ultimately found deceased. . . . Well, I couldn't order the defendants to accept a dead person to their seminary. If she's found alive, then the circumstances of her disappearance will then be known."

Looking straight at Tommy Riley, the judge said, "Depending upon the circumstances of her disappearance, I would be then able to rule on injunctive relief." The implications were clear: if Tommy had hidden her and he had a jury verdict in her favor, Judge Bateman wasn't going to rule until she was found. The reason for her disappearance had better have been outside of Tommy's or Allie's control.

"As a result, these proceedings are adjourned until nine tomorrow morning. Let us all hope that the task force is successful in determining the whereabouts of Ms. Batista. I'll see you gentlemen in the morning," Judge Bateman said.

As Tommy and Renzulli prepared to leave the judge's chambers, Renzulli seemed lost in thought. As they closed the doors behind them, he blurted, "Mr. Riley, a word please."

Tommy turned. "Sure, Monsignor, but quickly. I'm going to ride around with the task force."

"Certainly," said Renzulli, still in a daze. He grabbed hold of Tommy's arm with an urgency that got his attention. "Listen, I hope you realize that we had nothing to do with this, this disappearance."

"I know you didn't, Renzulli. You guys are evil but you're not that evil. And to be 100 percent honest with you, it doesn't really concern me whether she becomes a priest or not. Do I want to win? Sure. Nothing would make me happier professionally than kicking your Harvard butt in that courtroom. But I just want her safe. I've never met anyone like her, and you'd say the same thing, too, if you took the time to know her."

Renzulli still looked as though he was in a trance. "I'm sure you're right. Too bad I never had the chance. What is it about her, Mr. Riley?"

"A wise woman, her name is Nikki, told me last week that I don't have any faith. This is a true fact. Not only do I not have faith, I scorn it. I actively mock it. But no longer. Allie showed even a faithless heathen like me that it's okay to believe in something, even if it's totally irrational. Even if it's superstitious hocus-pocus. You guys believe, sure. But you're also paid to believe. On some level, you're part of a big machine. I met someone who has more faith than anyone, who has no incentive to believe. And all I can say is your Church," he grinned, "*our* Church, is missing out. I'll be going now."

Renzulli grabbed him by the arm again, this time surprising Tommy a great deal. The Monsignor had troubling thoughts floating through his brain, thoughts he couldn't enunciate and hardly dared to face. Finally, he blurted out, "I'll pray for her. For both of you." He released his grip.

Tommy thanked him, but all he could think about was the twenty-four hours they had to find Alejandra Batista. Tommy prayed as well that she was unhurt. He hadn't prayed since the third grade. He was rusty on some of the specifics, but he knew that Allie would appreciate the gesture.

CHAPTER FORTY-ONE

Tommy and Silk arrived back at the office to find that the off-duty policemen had their hands full with the media. Tommy assumed, and rightly so, that the task force had put Allie's picture out to TV stations. Tommy decided to use the opportunity to aid the search for Allie. He began by addressing the cameras directly.

"I have a statement I'd like to make."

There was immediate silence.

"Alejandra Batista is missing, and it is our highest priority to bring her home unharmed. The Gulf Coast Task Force has been initiated to find her. If anyone has any information at all regarding her whereabouts, please call the New Orleans Police Department and ask for Lieutenant Sam Pierce.

"This is not a ploy on our part to gain sympathy from the jury. Nor do I believe the Catholic Church is involved in any way. This is a very real emergency. Obviously kidnapping is a distinct possibility in this case, given the passions on either side of the debate. If anyone suspects someone they know might be behind something like this, we ask that you call the New Orleans Police Department. That's all I have. Thank you."

Tommy immediately turned and walked into the office, followed by Willis. The ever-present Betty was there, but they dispensed with the pleasant banter they usually enjoyed.

Silk and Tommy collapsed on chairs in Tommy's office. They hadn't been able to take a breath since the day started. Finally, Silk leaned forward.

"Tommy, what you said out there gave me an idea," Willis began. "I agree that the official Catholic Church would not be involved in this. But what about extremist factions?"

Tommy thought a moment and picked up his intercom, asking Betty to call Monsignor Renzulli.

A few minutes later, Betty rang on the intercom. "Monsignor Renzulli is holding for you, boss."

Tommy picked up the phone and said, "Hello, Monsignor Renzulli." Without waiting for a reply, he continued. "I'll get right to the point. Is the Church aware of any extremist fringe groups here in the New Orleans area?"

There was a long silence before Monsignor Renzulli answered. "I have a few leads. I was going to mention it at the courthouse but . . . It's delicate but we're working on it. Let me make some calls, Mr. Riley. I'll get back to you as quickly as possible."

"Thank you, Monsignor," Tommy said, genuinely appreciative.

"And Mr. Riley, I appreciate what you said to the media. Thank you," Renzulli said.

"Of course," Tommy replied, and hung up.

Thirty anxious minutes later, Renzulli rang back.

"There's a church outside the city. They call themselves the Society of Saint Pius X," the Monsignor began. "It's an offshoot of a Swiss priory that went astray about 40 years ago. The pastor is a right-wing zealot by the name of Lefebvre. They reject Vatican II, say the Mass in Latin, and require women to have their heads covered—pretty much everything the Church did before reform. Having said all that, they're mostly above board, nothing illegal. But if there's a group like you asked about, Father Lefebvre might know where to look."

"Thanks, Monsignor," Tommy replied. "Can I ask a favor?"

"Please," Renzulli replied.

"I don't have the best reputation among Catholic priests these days. Would you consider setting up an appointment for me?"

After a moment Renzulli said, "He would never refuse my request. If you leave now for his office, I'll let him know you're on the way."

"Thank you, Monsignor," Tommy replied.

"Good luck. I'm praying for both of you," Renzulli responded and hung up.

CHAPTER FORTY-TWO

The Society of Saint Pius X was located on the outskirts of the city in Metairie. Tommy and Silk parked well down the street to avoid suspicion. They brushed aside a curtain of Spanish moss hanging from a 300-year-old oak, dating back to the original French-Canadian settlers. Hurricane Katrina destroyed millions of trees, but nearly every single live oak survived. After centuries in place they were so well adapted to their environment, thought Tommy as he ran his fingers through the lush moss, they could weather any storm that nature could inflict. He hoped to procure the verdict that would help the even older Catholic Church survive its future as well. Without Allie, though, that would be impossible.

Father Lefebvre sat behind his desk with his hands folded in front of him, wearing an annoyed scowl.

As Tommy and Silk began introductions, the priest raised his hand for silence and got right to the point. As Tommy faced the renegade priest, Silk admired the leather tomes that lined the walls.

"I detest what you're trying to do, Mr. Riley. You're putting a fly in the ointment where there was no fly. Female priests.

I would not have granted this audience without the Monsignor's intervention."

Silk turned and mockingly mouthed the word "Audience?" behind the priest's back.

"But he seems to think this woman's life might be in danger," Father Lefebvre said. "I believe in my mission here. But if we lose sight of Christ's teachings, what's the use? At a certain point, we're Christians first and then Catholics. So how can I help?"

"Father, whoever abducted Ms. Batista did it for one purpose only: to stop her from becoming a priest. I know the Catholic Church would not be involved in something like this, nor would it sanction these horrible actions. But whoever did this probably has some affiliation, because only a Catholic would have an interest in stopping her." Tommy knew he would need to finesse the next part. "It could be the work of an extremist fringe group."

"Mr. Riley," Father Lefebvre's face reddened, "if you mean to insinuate—"

Tommy took a deep breath and said quickly, "These people would be extremely conservative in their approach to Catholicism. They would reject the changes of Vatican II, for example, as your parish does. We think it's possible they would come to Pius X to receive the Eucharist. It's not a reflection on you, Father."

Father Lefebvre felt his temperature rising but tried to remain calm. "How dare you suggest that one of my parishioners could be involved in something as terrible as this," he said.

"Not at all. I'm merely suggesting that someone whose beliefs are twisted would think they were doing God's work by abducting Ms. Batista. It's reasonable to assume they would prefer to hear the Mass in Latin. I don't believe that any sane member of your congregation would want to put her life in jeopardy. But time is of the essence right now, so I beg you to put hurt feelings aside."

"We get plenty of troubled souls through these doors; it comes with the territory. But it's not like we ask for I.D. Anyone is free to worship here as they please. If you come back Sunday—"

"I'm sorry, Father, but we don't have any time to waste. A faithful woman is in danger."

"Faithful?" Lefebvre roared. "Fly in the ointment. I'm sorry, gentlemen, but I can't offer you any assistance. I simply have no idea. Good day."

Silk turned from the bookshelves for the first time since he had entered.

"You've got quite the collection here."

He pulled one especially ornate volume off the shelf. Tommy noticed that the book was in Latin.

"*The Canonical Path of Opus Dei*. You follow Opus Dei as well?"

The renegade priest looked up. "Your command of Latin is impressive for a . . ." He paused as he stared at Silk and finally drawled, "lawyer."

Silk smirked. "It's not that difficult. Cramming theology is no different than cramming for the bar exam. How about I quiz you. 'Ye shall know them by their fruits.' Well?"

Lefebvre answered, "Matthew 7:16. What's your point?"

Silk walked to the desk to face Lefebvre.

"You said you were a Christian first. Look, I know you can't possibly know every single person that comes in here. But think beyond Mass. Think beyond confession. I know you do community outreach, for example."

Lefebvre replied, "Mr. Thompson, we can't counsel troubled souls without some form of anonymity. Believe me, if I knew anything I would tell you."

Silk had an idea. "Fair enough. What about an organization that's more extreme than yours? What about these Palmarians?"

Lefebvre laughed. "You've done your research. Mr. Riley, whatever you pay him it's not enough. They're mostly concentrated in Spain, where the true heretics live."

Tommy stepped in. "Thank you, Father. We need to leave before I can't afford Christmas bonuses this year."

Silk handed Father Lefebvre their cards. The Father set them down immediately on the desk.

"Wait a minute. There was a guy. I thought he was Spanish," Lefebvre drifted off.

"Go on Father," Tommy replied. "Anything you can give us."

"He used to come to every single Mass."

"So he was religious. My grandmother used to go to Mass three or four times a week," said Tommy.

"He came three or four times on Sundays alone. And he was a young man. He told me he had applied to the seminary many times but was never accepted. Clearly it was for psychological reasons. He hasn't been here for, I don't know—well over a year."

"That's something," Tommy said, "but it isn't much."

"Father," Silk cut in, "you said he was Spanish."

"No," Father Lefebvre relied. "I said I thought he was Spanish. But he was French."

"What's his name?"

"I have no idea."

Tommy's patience had evaporated. "Silk, let's go. We have no time for this."

"I just saw him, though. Last week, I was in the city to stop by the Archdiocese. I'm used to some protesters with all the scandal; I usually don't pay any mind. But I saw him on the sidewalk outside, holding a sign. It said, 'Associates of the Lamb of God.' The weird thing is, he was wearing a priest's cassock."

"Would you be able to identify him?" Tommy inquired.

"Certainly. But wait a minute," Father Lefebvre stood. His mind was working overtime trying to formulate something. "I went inside and I asked the young priest at the desk, you know, 'Is he one of ours?' He shook his head. And then he mouthed something—I thought he said, 'Excommunicated.'"

Silk looked at Tommy. "So he's kicked out. How does that help us?"

Tommy grabbed Silk's arm as he was halfway out the door. "They keep records of everything. That means he's on file. Father, get the Monsignor on the phone, please. We want to know of any Frenchmen excommunicated within the last year. I'm guessing it's not a big list. Get me those names. And thank you."

CHAPTER FORTY-THREE

In the car on the way back to the city, Tommy and Willis researched the Associates of the Lamb of God. The organization maintained a blog, which consisted of rantings and ravings in large, garish fonts. The blog listed radical changes to the Catholic Church they wanted implemented, with accompanying scriptural and historical references. Tommy noticed an especially long rant against female priests, but then nothing for the past week.

Five minutes after they left, Tommy's cell phone rang. Tommy was surprised to recognize the number. "Hello, Renzulli," he answered.

Renzulli was abrupt. "Whatever you said to Father Lefebvre, let's just say he's not a fan. But he seemed adamant that there was a link to this Frenchman. Riley, this list is highly confidential. If it gets out, I could well find my name on it."

Tommy took the plea seriously. "I know it is, Monsignor, and I wouldn't ask unless it was life or death. I will never divulge it to anyone. You have my word as a lawyer and a Catholic."

Renzulli responded, "Good enough. I'm sending it to you now. We tried grouping the French names at the top, but it's impossible—this is New Orleans. There's no mention of citizenship either. I sent the full list going back two years, but it's well over 100 names. In the meantime, I'm making inquiries of those who work here. But it must be discreet so it won't be quick. If I have anything, I'll text you. Good luck and Godspeed."

It was even more confusing than Renzulli had indicated. The list had 21 French names that had been excommunicated and removed from the rolls. Nine women on the list had terminated pregnancies, and three men and three women were doctors who had performed pregnancy terminations. Tommy and Silk crossed them off the list. From their LinkedIn pages, they learned that two more men were registered nurses, and one was a pharmacist.

"They certainly have a type," Tommy pointed out. "Anything medical we can cross off."

Of the three remaining men, two had been ordained as priests decades earlier. That left one man, Jean Boudreaux. "It's gotta be him," Silk exclaimed. But their enthusiasm waned when they learned that Boudreaux had been incarcerated at Angola six months earlier for committing racially-motivated crimes.

"Dammit," said Tommy. "What are we missing?"

"We've still got the full list. Let's divide it up. I'll start with the A's; you start with the M's," said Silk.

Tommy shook his head. "We don't have time. I'm going to call the office to help run these down. It could take all day."

Tommy reached for his phone. "Betty, it's me. . . . Not well. . . . No, we don't. . . . No, nothing. . . . Listen, we need all hands on deck. I've got about 130 possibilities; I need everyone online looking for any possible info."

"I think I've got him," Silk said quietly, lost in thought.

"We're looking for a young-ish French male who's not a nurse or doctor and not an ordained priest."

"I've got him," Silk said confidently.

"I need you, Danielle, Randi, Gerald—anyone you can find. I'm sending the list now—"

"Tommy, hang up the phone," Silk said firmly.

Tommy stared at Silk. "I gotta call you back," said Tommy, putting the phone down. "So?"

"He's right there in the As. It's an Irish name but I see his game. You don't play chess with the grandmaster and expect to keep all your pieces. Michael Agnew. He's the guy."

"How do you know?"

"Come on Tommy, Agnew? Agneau. Agneau is French for lamb."

They soon found a picture of Michael Agnew online—rail thin, balding, with deep-set brown eyes and a thick beard. And just as Father Lefebvre had described him, he was wearing a priest's cassock. When Silk saw the photo, he nearly jumped out of his skin.

"I know this guy!" Willis said. "He's part of the press corps. He's been in the courtroom every minute of the trial. He must have gotten credentials from some lunatic blog. He hasn't been wearing the robe, but that's him."

"Let's try the Irish Channel," Tommy said. "Why make up an Irish name unless you're surrounded by Paddys. My own people—I love the irony."

They noted the address of the Associates of the Lamb of God headquarters. Sure enough, it was just off Tchoupitoulas Street by the river—in the heart of the old Irish neighborhood.

Tommy called the New Orleans Police Department looking for Sam Pierce.

While he was on hold, Tommy hung up the phone. "Silk, did you ever get your permit to carry?"

Silk rolled his eyes. "No, and I never will. Tommy, what's

on your mind now?" It wasn't a question, as much as an admission that his boss had come to a decision.

Tommy's voice grew quiet as he imagined the worst. "This guy Agnew. He's. He's a martyr, an extremist. The only positive outcome for this guy is to make sure Allie never enters the seminary. Ever."

"Tommy, you're trying my patience. Get the cops back on the phone."

"I will, Silk, I will. But if you were looking for something, something very delicate, would you send the New Orleans P.D. into your old neighborhood in Tremé?"

Silk thought hard about how to steer Tommy in a different direction. But even he was speechless. "In this city, hell no. Fine, what's your plan?"

Tommy called forward to the front seat. "Manny, have you taken the nine millimeter out to the range recently? And do you have it with you?"

"Every week boss. Shoots low and to the right, maybe an inch at 15 yards. But it's so consistent, I just leave it. I always carry it with me."

Tommy turned back to Silk. "Most of my dad's old friends are gone. But not all of them," he said. And he picked up the phone.

Ten minutes later, they pulled up one block from the headquarters of the Associates of the Lamb of God.

CHAPTER FORTY-FOUR

The Irish Channel was an old residential neighborhood just a few miles up the Mississippi River from the French Quarter. Though close in proximity, it was worlds apart. It had attracted thousands of immigrants in the 19th century, attractive due to its higher elevation—protection against the ubiquitous New Orleans flooding. It had mostly survived Hurricane Katrina and was beloved for its traditional old shotgun houses.

But with the recent resurgence of inner-city living, new construction had sprung up next to old. With the affluent living among the less fortunate, the neighborhood was a melting pot of cultures and housing design. The building that headquartered the Associates of the Lamb of God was a small, single-story bungalow of gray adobe. It looked like some of the other old homes on the street except for a magnificent cross that stood atop the tiled roof over the porch. Even with the cross, it blended in.

From the relative safety of his car, Tommy looked at the structure down the street.

"Good to see the entire neighborhood hasn't gentrified yet," he said. "Anywhere else, this building would stick out like a sore thumb."

Almost as if on cue, an old black Cadillac flashed the lights twice and pulled up alongside them. The younger driver put it in park and an old man with white, bushy eyebrows leaned his head out.

Tommy grinned wide when he saw him. "Hello, Seamus, you look well."

A thick Irish lilt rang out from inside the Caddy. "Tommy, you know I'd do anything for your father. But I don't mind saying it to yer face—a woman in the priesthood? Sheer blasphemy."

Tommy chuckled, "Thanks for your opinion, Seamus, but that's for the court to decide. In the meantime, I think she's in there. What can you tell me?"

"Hard to tell; it's pretty dark. Alarm in back and one in front as well. Go through the back door; we disabled it. Front door you'll get the bells and whistles but no alarm service—no line to the cops."

"What does the lock look like on the back door?" Tommy asked. "Do you think the two of us can break it down?"

It was Seamus' turn to chuckle, "Save your strength, Tommy boy. We unlocked it for you." The old man nodded and the black Cadillac drove off.

Silk looked at Tommy. "I thought your father was a bartender. You didn't tell me he was in the IRA."

"He wasn't, Silk, he wasn't. But he certainly hosted his fair share of meetings in the back room. Let's go."

"Tommy, what if he isn't here?" Willis asked.

"Then we go to Plan B," Tommy said cryptically.

"Which is?"

"Silk, you sound like a lawyer," Tommy said, climbing out of the car.

CHAPTER FORTY-FIVE

As the old Irishman had promised, the back door opened with a soft click. They stepped into the kitchen and scanned the room. It was spotless.

"Either this guy is very neat or he wasn't here last night," Willis said.

They walked into a small living area, which was also quite tidy.

The house was silent as a tomb as they quietly moved through.

Glancing at a desk in the living room, Tommy spotted a pile of articles cut out of newspapers and magazines about the lawsuit Allie had filed against the Church. A yellow highlighter had been used to identify comments in the articles that were detrimental to the Church. There was no doubt left—Tommy was positive he had found his man. Carefully, Tommy sifted through the drawers and found a utility bill addressed to Michel Vachon at an address he did not recognize.

"Who's Michel Vachon?" Tommy mused.

"I think we found our Frenchman," Silk intoned.

"I know where she is," Tommy said, "let's go." He showed Silk the bill as he moved to the front of the house. He highlighted the address then folded the bill neatly and placed it on a table in the foyer.

As Tommy went to open the front door, Silk stopped him.

"Tommy, wait! The alarm will go off if you walk out that door."

Without any hesitation at all, Tommy opened the door and the alarm immediately sounded.

"This is Plan B," Tommy smiled. "The address is in the Warehouse District. Let's go!"

As the Navigator tore down Tchoupitoulas Street, Tommy heard the sound of the alarm grow fainter and fainter.

CHAPTER FORTY-SIX

The phone rang and Tommy picked it up. "Riley."

"Hello, Tommy, it's Lieutenant Pierce. I just got off the phone with Monsignor Renzulli. They've got a hunch about a guy—crazy priest who lives in the Irish Channel. I'm going to send a cruiser out there to see what they can find. Stay away from this, Tommy. We've got it from here," Pierce said determinedly.

"Of course, Lieutenant," Tommy said, unconvincingly.

"You're on your way there, aren't you?" Pierce asked.

"Yep," Tommy lied.

Pierce paused. "Just don't do anything until the officers get there. If she's there, you may wind up causing her harm if you interfere. Understand? I mean it Tommy."

As soon as Sam Pierce hung up the phone, Tommy turned to Silk.

"We bought ourselves some time but not much. Manny, step on it. And hand me the nine. Low and to the right?"

"That's right, boss. Low and to the right." Manny reached into the glove box and handed a Smith & Wesson nine-millimeter pistol to the back seat.

†

They arrived at the warehouse. Manny parked the Navigator cautiously a block away.

Tommy and Willis walked around the building and found a steel door on the east side. The chain and padlock looked fairly new and heavy enough not to be compromised unless cut with a heavy-duty bolt cutter. Further inspection of the latch indicated that the rivets attaching the latch to the door were old and rusted. Tommy thought he could possibly break the latch free from the building if he had a strong piece of metal to pry it off. He returned with a tire iron to the building and with one swift jerk, the latch popped off with the padlock and chain intact. He turned to Silk. *That was easy.*

"Maybe we should wait for the cops," Willis whispered. The look on Tommy's face said it all.

"We're not gonna wait for the cops, are we?" Silk said.

"Nope," Tommy responded, resolute.

The empty warehouse was dark except for the sunlight filtering through the open door. It had an unusual odor that Tommy thought could be burning wax. In the dim light, they saw some kind of office enclosure.

From behind, they heard the sound of a cat landing on the lid of a trash can. The lid fell to the ground with a clatter. As Tommy and Willis turned back toward the sound, a shrill scream suddenly pierced the silence. The blood curdling shriek froze Silk to the spot, but it gave Tommy hope. "She's alive," he whispered, drawing the weapon. He pointed to the door, and Silk nodded, relieved to finally do something physical.

"I'm going to knock that thing down like a five-foot-ten point guard," he said, as he lowered his shoulder and charged the door.

CHAPTER FORTY-SEVEN

Tommy and Willis burst into the room. They were momentarily disoriented by a glowing horizon of candles that filled the stale air with a musky odor. They squinted to adjust their eyes to the flickering light.

Beyond the eerie glare, they saw movement—the silhouette of a black-robed figure holding a gruesome leather whip high above another figure in a contorted position. Allie! She was bent forward with her wrists shackled and her head on a piece of wood, exposing her neck. Even by candlelight, Tommy could see she was barely conscious and bleeding badly.

"Put the weapon down!" Tommy yelled.

Responding to the intruders, the black-robed figure turned to face them. He flung the leather whip aside and said simply, "Welcome, Mr. Riley. But this heretic has not yet confessed her sins. You will be witness to the Associates of the Lamb of God."

Tommy had been shooting since he was a Boy Scout, and was a crack shot with a handgun. But nothing had prepared him for the high stakes of this moment. As Vachon spoke, Tommy searched frantically for an open shot. Allie's prostrate body blocked most of his angles. The murderous priest's head was too close to Allie's, but he noticed Vachon's left knee protruding from the robe at a safe distance below the torture table. He took a deep breath, let it all out, then held it and said softly to himself, "Low and to the right."

Suddenly, Vachon grabbed a large, curved saber. Raising the weapon above Allie's exposed neck, he cried, "God's will be done!"

He had barely finished the sentence when a deafening shot rang out, and the smell of cordite filled the air. With a loud crack and the ping of metal hitting the hard wood contraption, the sword was released from Vachon's hands as he fell writhing to the floor, the weapon missing Allie's head by inches.

Tommy was so shocked that it took him several moments to realize that he hadn't even fired his weapon. All he could feel was the pounding of adrenaline in his veins; all he could hear was the sound of his heart beating in his ears. Even as he stared around the room he wasn't sure what to make of the colossal gift he had received. Still, he held the gun aloft in an aggressive posture, unsure of what his eyes and ears were trying to tell him. Finally, he heard the reassuring voice of Silk who put his hand on the barrel of the gun, slowly lowering it to the floor. "Tommy," he said, "it's over."

The entire warehouse was swarming with police officers. As Tommy saw Lieutenant Sam Pierce approaching, he finally realized they had all been saved and bent to the floor to slowly place his weapon on the ground.

"You have a license to carry that thing?" the Lieutenant drawled.

Tommy, still dazed, reached for his wallet. "Of course, I—"

Lieutenant Pierce just smiled. "Relax. We're here. Go to your client."

As Tommy walked past him, he noticed blood rhythmically pulsing from Vachon's knee. *That was the shot,* he thought. And he was sure glad someone else had taken it.

†

Allie's soft, rhythmic sobs had been muffled until the terrifying silence of that moment.

Tommy saw her then, covered in blood. He rushed toward her and gently reached down to her. "Allie, can you hear me?"

She stirred in reply.

"Allie, help is here," he said gently. "You're going to be okay."

She opened her eyes, if only barely—and for a fleeting moment Tommy saw the look of resolve, the one he had witnessed time and time again.

Tommy held her hand and wouldn't let go, even while the paramedics took care of her.

"Thank God," Tommy whispered. "Thank God."

CHAPTER FORTY-EIGHT

"Where are you taking her?" Tommy asked the paramedics.

"Charity Hospital," one of the emergency technicians said.

Tommy finally stepped out of the way as more police units roared into the parking lot. Tommy had no intention of sticking around. But Allie remained his top priority. Willis was two steps ahead when he pulled up alongside him in the Navigator. As the pair sped off, Tommy dialed a number on his phone. A baritone voice piped up on the other line.

"Tommy! What's a celebrity like you calling me for?"

Without any preamble, Tommy blurted, "Don, we've found Alejandra Batista. She's on her way to Charity Hospital."

"I'll be there in ten minutes," Don said immediately and hung up.

Don Erwin had been the right tackle on the Tulane football team and was a bear of a man. He had studied pre-med, followed by a degree from the UT Medical School. Don was one of the preeminent surgeons in New Orleans, if not in Louisiana; he and his wife, Malone, were among Tommy's best friends. Tommy knew Allie would be in the best of hands with Don calling the shots.

Manny dropped Tommy off at the ER before he took Silk home. Inside, he went right for the first nurse he saw, dispensing with introductions.

"Paramedics are bringing in Alejandra Batista, and she's hurt badly. Dr. Don Erwin will be here very shortly, and I want him to be in charge of her triage and ultimate care." Handing her an American Express Black Card, he finished. "Any questions?"

"No, sir, but you hold on to that," the woman responded simply, handling Tommy back his credit card. "Everything has to go through insurance."

Tommy turned just as Allie was being wheeled in by the paramedics on a gurney. He turned to the nurse, noticing her name tag.

"Nurse Romero, I trust you to take care of Ms. Batista until Dr. Erwin gets here. Will you please do that?"

She responded with another "Yes, sir," and moved toward Allie and the paramedics.

CHAPTER FORTY-NINE

Judge Bateman addressed the jury the next morning.

"While I assume none of you have been watching news reports, as you've been instructed, I feel the need to acknowledge that some or all of you may have heard that the plaintiff, Alejandra Batista, was abducted as a result of this case by someone meaning her harm. I'm pleased to tell you that she has been found."

The jurors traded glances, relieved.

"The man responsible for her abduction had no affiliation with anyone involved in this lawsuit, including the defendants or the Catholic Church. Do you understand this? If so, please say yes."

"Yes, Your Honor," the six jurors nodded and responded.

"She will not be available to appear in court today," Judge Bateman continued. "This, again, is not a reflection on the Catholic Church or the defendants. Do you understand this? Again, if you do understand, please say yes.'"

"Yes, Your Honor," they responded.

"Very well. Now we begin the closing argument. The plaintiff's counsel, Mr. Riley, will first argue how he believes the testimony you have heard is relevant to the position of his client. Next, the defendants' counsel, Monsignor Renzulli, will argue how the testimony is relevant to the position of his clients. Then I will give you certain instructions before you retire to the jury room. Once in the jury room, you will consider answers to the questions I will also give to you. You'll select a foreman or forewoman from among you to answer on behalf of all of you when you have reached a unanimous verdict. Does anyone have any questions?"

When there were none, Judge Bateman said, "Mr. Riley, you may now address the jury."

Tommy stood up and clasped his hands in front of him as he faced the jury.

"Shortly, the six of you will go into the jury room and be asked to decide unanimously the answers to two questions. Do the defendants discriminate against Alejandra Batista solely on the basis of her gender, by denying her the right to attend a seminary in their jurisdiction to study for the priesthood? If your answer is yes, then you will have to answer the next question. Do the defendants have *justifiable* cause to exclude her because of her gender?

"Let's talk about the first question. You've heard sworn testimony that a candidate for the seminary and a candidate for the priesthood *must* be an unmarried male baptized and confirmed in the Catholic Church. I submit that is discriminatory behavior on its face. Those qualifications specifically exclude women, regardless of merit. Period, end of story."

Tommy looked at each juror one by one and continued. "You have heard sworn testimony that Alejandra Batista has every other qualification to be a priest by Dr. Turner, one of the psychologists contracted by the defendants to verify the qualifications of the candidates for the seminary and priesthood. That's Alejandra Batista the *person*, not the woman or the man, but the *person*. The only thing she lacks to be a priest in the eyes of the defendants is male genitalia. I repeat, that is the *only* thing she lacks, and that is the part of the anatomy that a priest is forbidden to use in a sexual manner and is therefore irrelevant to the qualifications. It is clear she has been discriminated against solely because of her gender.

"I will also point out that the defendants have ordained *married* males who obviously do not meet their own qualifications of an *unmarried* male. They claim they have special reasons for doing this. And yet when asked whether a female who falls within those special circumstances could be ordained as well, they answered no because she is still a woman. The defendants ordain men, married and unmarried, which is clear. But they will not ordain a woman no matter what, and that is also clear. The defendants clearly undertake a discriminatory practice based solely upon the gender of the person,.

"Now let's talk about the second question. Do the defendants have *justifiable* cause to exclude women, such as the plaintiff, from the seminary and the priesthood? The defendants claim they have justifiable cause because Jesus Christ appointed only men, not women, as His apostles. It's their position that by not appointing a woman, Jesus meant to exclude women forever from the priesthood. In order for their argument to have any validity at all, the *only* reason must be that He meant one act of omission to forever prevent women from joining the priesthood.

"If there's any *other* reason that caused him to appoint men only at that time, their argument fails. If there are three or four or even more reasons why He did not appoint a woman as an apostle . . . well, you can see the foundation upon which they have built their argument is built on sand. All you need to do is find *one* valid reason why He did not name a woman as an apostle at that time, other than to forever prevent women from becoming a priest, and their foundation crumbles. Unfortunately for the defendants, there are many more reasons than one.

"Let's take a look at the times and circumstances in which Jesus appointed His apostles. Their number was twelve, corresponding with the twelve tribes of Israel as you have heard from the testimony.

"You also heard there had never been a head of a tribe who was a woman, and that to maintain that tradition Jesus Christ would have appointed only men. That was the tradition and that's what He would have done. Did He mean that men only were to be priests forever? Did He mean that with the passage of time and when His new religion expanded and broke from the Hebrew tradition, women were to be excluded forever from the priesthood? I don't think so. Once this initial and seemingly valid reason for appointing men no longer existed, what would have been the point?"

Tommy took some time to let his points sink in by pretending to look at his notes, then he looked up again and directed a sincere gaze to the jury.

"There are other reasons why He might not have appointed a woman as an apostle. You have heard testimony that women at the time were little more than slaves. At the time of Jesus Christ, no woman could hold a leadership position, period."

Tommy was just getting started. "Jesus Christ was not on earth to undertake social reform. He didn't do that with slavery and other social norms that He disagreed with. And He didn't do it when He appointed men, exclusively, as priests.

"The apostles also had characteristics other than being male, such as being Jewish and married. The defendants dismiss these other characteristics as incidental and not fundamental. The defendants dismiss *any* characteristic the apostles had except for one, their gender. They claim that these other characteristics were incidental in light of the social times in which Jesus lived. Yet they ignore the social custom of the taboo against women, which was very prevalent in those times. Are they talking out of both sides of their mouths? I'll let you answer that for yourselves.

"Let's talk about how being Jewish and married is incidental. Those characteristics seemed pretty fundamental to me. Ask yourselves about your own marital status and ethnic roots. They deal directly with your family and your family heritage. How fundamental are they to you? Can the defendants merely dismiss these as being incidental and not fundamental any more than gender is fundamental? I don't think so.

"The characteristics of the apostles were all the same. If any of them were fundamental, then they all had to be fundamental. If any of them were incidental, then they were all incidental. How can anyone, two thousand years later, pick and choose among the characteristics of the apostles and determine which Jesus meant to last *forever* and disregard the rest as incidental?"

Tommy continued, "However, the characteristics were *all*, and I repeat *all*, incidental to the times in which Jesus Christ lived. Nothing more, nothing less. He didn't mean that a priest should be Jewish forever. He didn't want to rock the boat of Jewish hierarchy by appointing a Gentile at the time. He didn't mean that all priests forever should be married. And He did not mean that priests should be males forever. He didn't want to rock the boat of a male-dominated society by appointing a woman at the time. The characteristics common to the apostles were determined by the customs of those times, nothing more and nothing less.

"As time passed and those customs evolved, the characteristics required by those customs were no longer required. Opposing counsel would have you believe that certain men called popes are infallible, and the rules of the Church are inviolate, consistent, and unchanging. This simply couldn't be further from the truth. The clergy was commonly married until the Middle Ages. The Church didn't start enforcing the rules for religious reasons; they just didn't want a bunch of offspring squabbling over church property. Even then, the change was not made for scriptural reasons. It's foolish and unreasonable to read anything further into it other than that.

"Now let's talk about the two different instances in which women were present when both men and women received priestly powers from Jesus Christ: the Last Supper and the Pentecost. You heard testimony that says there is equal evidence to show that women were present on those occasions. If women were there, they received the same directions that the men did. If you believe what the defendants say, that Jesus Christ treated women equally with men, would He have excluded them from the Last Supper or the Pentecost?

"It doesn't sound like He would have. Jesus Christ wasn't around to run the early church after His death, and it seems clear that the men in control at that time would have excluded women from any leadership position because that's what *they* believed, not what *He* believed. While Jesus Christ excluded women from the initial apostles for social reasons, I believe a strong case can be made that just before His death and after His resurrection, He included women when He conferred the power of priesthood to His original twelve apostles.

"There is no scriptural evidence that says women were not there, and the actions of Jesus would indicate they most likely were there. The defendants will say this is entirely supposition and there is no direct Biblical evidence for the claim. I respond that the defendants' proposition that Jesus intended to have men only in the priesthood forever is entirely supposition as well, and there is no direct biblical evidence for that claim."

Once more, Tommy paused. His gaze to the jury became more intense. "That brings me to my last point. You heard testimony that the dogma of the Catholic Church is the infallible truth, which the defendants hold dear. Catholics are forbidden to believe otherwise. One dogma is that men and women are created equal, and another is that only males can be priests. Those dogmas are in direct contradiction to each other. So which one should we believe? The first dogma follows what Jesus Christ said and did. The second dogma is based upon what He didn't do. Which has the most weight? The one He taught—that men and women are equal in every respect? Or the one He didn't teach—that only a man can be a priest?"

Tommy looked up at the courtroom for effect and was pleased to see Nikki sitting near the front. He looked at her until she smiled back.

"To summarize, they say, 'We have looked back two thousand years and have concluded that of all the characteristics the apostles had, the only one which Jesus meant to last forever as a qualification for the priesthood is the male gender.' This theory has clearly no basis in fact."

Tommy moved closer to the jury now, strolling in front of the jury box. "Ladies and gentlemen of the jury, I have one more thing to add. Some of you may conjecture that we have undertaken this lawsuit out of opposition to the Catholic Church. This could not be further from the truth. I myself am a lifelong Catholic, and while at times I have been less diligent than others, I have never felt closer to the Church than I have the past few weeks. I have seen this institution up close. I have held it up to the light and seen it operate at a high level, and function in a way that few other organizations on earth could manage." Tommy stole a glance at Renzulli, who returned it with an icy glare.

"Most importantly, I have felt faith. Not my own faith, mind you, but the faith of others. Faith to effect change. Faith strong enough to change the world."

He came face to face with the front row of jurors. "Institutions do not survive because they are infallible. They survive because they adapt. When you see those old oak trees in City Park, they still stand today because they learned to survive. The Catholic Church is a survivor. They have had some problems lately, yes, but that's part of survival. Female priests are inevitable, whether it happens today or 20 years from now. Already, so-called heretic female priests are being ordained—in Germany, in Canada, in Scandinavia. Yes, they are not technically considered legitimate by the Vatican, but does that really matter to the communities they reinforce, to the people they instruct, to the needy they bless? The United States, this great country, should be the place where this movement gains legal and procedural traction. Where we can tell our daughters, if you want to be a priest, be a priest. Where all men, and most certainly all women, are created equal. And once that moment happens, this Church, this great oak, will have another tool that it needs for survival."

After a momentary pause he continued, "The evidence is clear on the first question. 'Do the defendants discriminate solely because of gender?' The only answer is yes. On the second question the answer is equally clear. 'Do the defendants have reasonable and justifiable cause to discriminate?' No!

There can be no other choice."

Tommy looked at them for a moment and then said quietly and sincerely, "I thank you, and most of all Alejandra Batista thanks you."

He turned and sat down. You could hear a pin drop.

CHAPTER FIFTY

"Monsignor Renzulli, you may now address the jury," Judge Bateman said.

"Thank you, Your Honor," Renzulli said. Turning to the jury, he said, "And I also wish to thank you for your diligence and attention. When you retire to the jury room, you will have to answer two questions put before you. Mr. Riley just reviewed them. Does the Church discriminate against women because of their gender? And if so, do they have a justifiable reason to do so? In fairness to my client, the question you have to answer in your own mind is whether my clients, the Archdiocese of New Orleans and Archbishop Sierra, are arbitrary and capricious in what they do. In other words, are they mean-spirited people?

"Do they believe their activities are justified, or do they act out of hatred and disrespect for women? Discriminatory behavior is born out of bias and prejudice that has no justifiable basis. In order for you to find for the plaintiff, you must believe that the preponderance of evidence conclusively shows my clients hate women and do not want them to be priests. That's what this case is really about.

"Ladies and gentlemen, my clients do not hate women.

The testimony shows without a doubt that the defendants justifiably believe that what they're doing is a direction from the example of Jesus Christ, not the hatred of, or the lack of respect for, women.

"Jesus Christ did not appoint a woman as an apostle. That is an indisputable fact. The twelve apostles were the first priests; there is no dispute about this. The church believes, and the scriptures show, the apostles were ordained as priests at the Last Supper.

"Counsel for the plaintiff suggests that women were also present at the Last Supper and that Jesus Christ granted the same ordination to the women who were there.

"I ask you, what women? What woman? Who were they, and where did they go? If any women had been ordained as priests, those women would have known they were ordained as priests! The twelve apostles would also have known those women had been ordained as priests because they, too, were there. Would those women have simply disappeared from the early church and the written scriptures? Would the apostles have ignored and disregarded those women if Jesus had ordained them? No, I don't think so.

"There's no evidence to suggest that women were present, but we know one thing. The twelve apostles were there. They were ordained by Jesus Christ, and all of them were men. That we know is true. That's the only thing about the Last Supper we know to be true."

Renzulli waited a moment and then continued. "Plaintiff's counsel argues over and over that there is no direct revelation in the scriptures that priests must be men, and that it is nonsense to rely on something Jesus didn't do and thus not do it forever. Is it really? Jesus didn't hurt others. That is something else He didn't do. Is it nonsense to think He wanted His followers to follow that example of not hurting others forever? Of course, it's not. To say a person can't set an example by not doing something is nonsense.

"Counsel for the plaintiff has suggested social norms would have dictated the selection of men by Jesus. I don't know whether you believe Jesus Christ was a God-made man or not, but my clients do. They believe that God, as man, could have appointed any woman He chose to be an apostle.

"The very definition of God is that He can do anything. Does anybody believe, for even one second, that God, with the unimaginable powers that only God can have, would be even minutely bothered by the social norms of the society? He could have easily appointed a woman but did not do so. The reason He did not was because He was establishing the basis of His future church on earth. Every fundamental thing Jesus did, or refrained from doing, is an example for all Christians to follow today—not incidental things He did, such as appointing apostles that were married or had beards. The apostles also spoke Aramaic and were uneducated. Some of them were also fisherman, and some of them may have had red hair, too. Who cares? Those were all incidental characteristics, and the plaintiff's counsel is trying to confuse you by saying all of those characteristics, along with the apostles' gender, are merely incidental. What can be more fundamental to any of us than our gender? It is what defines us all. It is as fundamental as one can get. He set fundamental examples in all ways, and today the Church still tries to follow each and every one. That we know is true."

Renzulli paused to indicate a change of thought, for effect, and continued. "The first apostles knew Jesus as well as you would know anyone with whom you lived for *three* years. They ate with him, slept in the same house with him, talked with and listened to him—were constantly with him for three whole years. Think about it. That's a long time.

"Ask yourselves, how well would you know someone if you did what they did with Jesus for three years? The answer is obvious. You would know him very, very well. After His death, when they had an opportunity to select another apostle, and when they had many highly qualified women to call upon, they chose a man who may not have even known Jesus Christ. The first mention of him in the scriptures is when He is appointed to replace Judas.

"The apostles, of all people, would have known what Jesus Christ would have wanted. They were tortured in horrible, unimaginable ways, and murdered for doing what they knew Jesus Christ wanted them to do. To think that they would not have done what He wanted because of a social norm? Preposterous. I don't believe it, and neither should you. Forget social norms of the time and any bias the apostles might have had against women, as the plaintiff's counsel suggests. If Jesus Christ would have wanted women to be ordained as Catholic priests, they would have *known* it and they would have *done* it!

"In the two thousand years since the time of Jesus, there have certainly been hundreds of thousands, maybe a million or more, of Catholic clergy who were and are now dedicated to doing Christ's work on earth. That's their only mission and goal in life. No wife, no children, no other pursuits to interfere with their focus. Their job is literally their life. Yes, there have been married priests and priests with children and probably priests from Mars. We're talking about an organization with over one billion members. Opposing counsel chooses to cherry-pick infinitesimal exceptions in an effort to persuade you. But I know you're smarter than that.

"Throughout history, since the time of Jesus, they have asked themselves many times the question that you are being asked to answer today. What was the will of Jesus? They have concluded absolutely that the Catholic Church is justified in excluding women from the priesthood. It would have been much easier to answer differently. They wouldn't have the controversy they have here today. They have prayed about it, researched it, discussed it, and looked at it in every way possible. They have consistently answered it as Christ would have wanted them to answer it. The priesthood is to forever be reserved for the male gender only. There has been no inconsistency in this teaching for two thousand years.

"Now I get to the question I raised when I first started. Each one of you must ask yourself, 'Are my clients, the archdiocese and Bishop Sierra, doing this arbitrarily without regard to anything other than their hatred and disrespect for women?' You met Bishop Sierra. Ask yourself, 'Is he sincere in not allowing women to the seminary out of good faith? Or is he just a mean guy who hates women?'" There were a few smiles from the jurors. Pausing, he said, "Remember, it doesn't matter if you believe what Catholics believe.

"Counsel has put a lot of smoke out there about reasons for what Jesus may or may not have done. It doesn't matter what others may believe or may not believe. What is relevant—and this is extremely important for you to understand—is whether my clients have justifiable reasons to believe the way *they* believe, and therefore act as they act.

"I believe the answer is obvious. My clients have determined that what they do is what is required of them by their faith and belief, and they cannot do otherwise. It's a justifiable belief that guides their activities. It's simply not true that they act arbitrarily and capriciously out of disrespect for women.

They have just cause and a reasonable basis for limiting the priesthood to males. That's the only answer possible under the preponderance of evidence. It unquestionably leads you to the one and only answer to the second jury question: yes.

"Opposing counsel conjured a memorable and poignant image of the mighty oak tree withstanding centuries of hurricanes. Bravo, counselor." Renzulli smirked at Tommy, but not without warmth.

"But think about it for a second. The reason the oak survives is its roots, buried deep beneath the soil. It takes centuries to build, but the oak survives because of this foundation. Your decision here today is very important indeed. But we are just men and women, on this earth for a short period of time. The Catholic Church has roots that will continue to grow in the soil until the end of time.

He paused as he looked directly at the jury. "Thank you, again."

With that, Monsignor Renzulli slowly turned and sat down.

CHAPTER FIFTY-ONE

Waiting on a jury was always hard, and he knew he could never get used to it. It was a total feeling of helplessness, and Tommy did not like being helpless. Some counsel read books and novels to pass the time. Depending on the nature of the case and the perceived time of deliberation the jury would need to decide, some counsel even retired to spas or mountain getaways. But Tommy thought that was a waste of time. Some counsel obsessed over things they had done or wished they had during the trial; Tommy thought that was a bigger waste of time. He remembered Joe Bob used to go to La Carafe for a Scotch, so Tommy decided to take a cue from his mentor. Tommy and Silk adjourned to a private booth at the Polo Club Lounge in the Windsor Court Hotel, where Tommy proposed a toast to Joe Bob. They clinked glasses of Macallan 18, neat. They'd had a long week and the toast felt more meaningful than it might have otherwise. Just as the pair deliberated ordering a third round, they got the call.

†

As Tommy walked into the courtroom, he felt a familiar presence watching over him. There, seated in the back row with her walker and a nurse, sat his mother. Tommy waved. She acknowledged him with a slight nod, but kept her gaze forward, lips pursed.

Back at the plaintiff's table, Tommy glanced at his watch and noticed it had been three hours and thirty-six minutes since the jury had retired to discuss the verdict. That was a long time for two jury questions. He guessed the lion's share of the jury's time was focused on the second question, "Do they have justifiable cause to exclude women from the seminary and priesthood?"

Any time a jury came back, Tommy would try to search their faces for clues as to the verdict. He could often tell by whom the jurors looked at when they first came back into the jury box.

The bailiff brought the jury in and seated them. The jurors alternately looked at Tommy and Monsignor Renzulli with no emotion. No clue whatsoever. Everyone was seated when the bailiff announced Judge Bateman's return.

"Ladies and gentlemen of the jury, have you reached a verdict?" Judge Bateman asked.

"We have, Your Honor," said Mr. Madapusi and he stood up. The other five jurors had selected the Hindu as the foreman. The foreman was typically elected because he or she had been a forcible presence in the jury room. Mr. Madapusi must have displayed a natural sense of leadership and Tommy thought the selection boded well for his case.

"Will the bailiff please bring me the written verdict of the jury?" requested Judge Bateman. After he received it, he read it without any emotion. Then he turned to the jury and asked the foreman, "Is this the unanimous verdict of the jury?"

"Yes, Your Honor," Mr. Madapusi answered.

Judge Bateman continued, "Concerning question number one, do you find that the defendants discriminate against women solely because of their gender by excluding them from the seminary in order to study for the Catholic priesthood? Yes or no? What is your answer?"

Mr. Madapusi replied, "Our answer to that question is yes, Your Honor. They discriminate against women solely because of their gender."

No surprise there, Tommy thought.

"Since you've answered question number one in the affirmative, you are required to answer question number two. Do you find the defendants have a justifiable basis to exclude women from the seminary in order to study for the Catholic priesthood solely because of their gender? Yes or no? What is your answer?"

Mr. Madapusi took a few moments and looked at his jury form, and the silence was deafening. Not a cough, not a shuffle of feet, not a sound. Then he looked up and stared straight at Tommy Riley and said, "Our answer to that question is . . . no, Your Honor. They do not have a justifiable basis."

Audible commotion moved through the courtroom as reporters rushed out the door. Tommy closed his eyes, thinking of Allie. Then he looked to the back row, but Luisa was no longer there.

Before Judge Bateman announced his decision, Silk pushed a note toward Tommy. "No surprise. Hinduism is the oldest religion on earth. They've been ordaining women now for 20 years."

CHAPTER FIFTY-TWO

There was a policeman seated in a chair outside Allie's hospital door, reading a magazine, which made Tommy feel good that Dr. Erwin had taken the necessary precautions. The man looked up as Tommy approached and nodded at him. Tommy nodded back and pushed the door open as quietly as he could. He noticed Allie was lying prone face down on the bed. He approached the bed and spoke quietly. "Allie?"

She was heavily bandaged, but the bruises on her face were already starting to disappear.

She opened her eyes and looked at him, mumbling drowsily, "Mr. Riley."

"She speaks," he said, smiling. Even though she was on painkillers and sedatives, he knew she would be back running trails in no time.

"The trial is over," Tommy replied softly.

She raised her head slightly and asked, "And?"

Tommy thought a moment and then said, "The jury said that the defendants did not have a justifiable basis to exclude you from the seminary."

"So, we were right?" Allie said, lying her head back down.

"Yes, Allie, we were right," Tommy replied.

"So I can enroll in the seminary?" Allie asked earnestly.

Tommy looked out the window at the setting sun and thought it had been a very long day. Turning back to Allie, he softly said, "No, Allie, I'm afraid not."

"Why not?" she asked, lifting her head again slightly, confused. "I thought we prevailed on both matters?"

Tommy looked back at Allie with a calmness he did not feel. "We did. But there was a third issue we had to win to force the defendants to accept you to the seminary.

"It was left to Judge Bateman to decide whether or not to grant a mandatory injunction to require them to accept you. A mandatory injunction is available only when the plaintiff has no other adequate remedies available. I argued that the only available remedy for you as a Catholic was to become a Catholic priest.

"Monsignor Renzulli argued that there were many other Christian faiths that accepted women to their seminaries to study for the priesthood, and your own testimony supported that. Therefore, he argued, there are a number of other remedies available to you in order for you to become a priest in a Christian religion, other than Catholic."

Tommy again looked out the window. He noticed the sun had finished its journey of the day and was below the horizon.

After a moment, he turned back to Allie and continued, "When Judge Bateman rendered his decision, he said, 'If one believes in God, then by the very definition of God there can only be one God.' Then he said, 'If one believes that Jesus Christ was the son of God, then there can only be one Jesus Christ.'" Tommy paused again and then continued, "Judge Bateman went on to say, 'If anyone is a Christian and worships Jesus Christ, then the only object of that worship is the *same* God-made man. All Christian denominations, even though they may do it in a different way, must, by definition, worship the same Jesus Christ. There is only one.'"

Tommy looked at Allie softly and continued, "Judge Bateman concluded his ruling by saying that if you wished to become a priest in a Christian religion, there were any number of them that would accept you. Since you have other remedies available to you, he found that a mandatory injunction was not available to you under the law. I'm sorry, Allie."

For a long few moments, Allie looked at Tommy with her deep amber eyes. "The jury said that we were right, Mr. Riley. We were right. The jury said so. We were right." She grabbed his hand tightly, closed her eyes peacefully, and fell asleep.

AUTHOR NOTE

The book you have just read is a work of fiction, nothing more and nothing less. In the interest of the story, I took a few liberties with some federal procedural and statutory law. However, concerning the arguments for and against the ordination of women in the Catholic Church, I attempted, to the best of my ability, to portray each one in the most objective way I could.

In July of 2010, the head of the Roman Catholic Church, Pope Benedict XVI, revised the Catholic Church's ecclesiastical laws and strengthened its in-house rules on sex abuse cases. But in doing so he also ruled that any priest caught ordaining women would be designated as having committed a *grave crime*. This is the same term used for a priest who engages in pedophilia.

While reasonable people could debate whether the horrors of pedophilia and the ordination of a female priest belong in the same category of an offense, what is clear and obvious, by making the comparison, is that the pope and the present hierarchy of the Catholic Church is intractable on whether women can be priests. Unless Pope Francis or another future pope amends this law, it will forever remain the law of the Roman Catholic Church.

What few polls that have been taken of American Catholics about the issue have resulted in an almost even split. It is a highly-charged topic in the United States today, with no room for compromise of opinions. However, the Catholic Church is not an institution of the people, by the people, or for the people since the Catholic Church is not a democracy but an autocracy, albeit a benevolent one. As such, it appears highly unlikely that the Holy See will ever be influenced by the opinion of one, some, or all of the over one-billion Catholics in the world.

I hope you enjoyed the story.

—Roger A. Brown

CPSIA information can be obtained
at www.ICGtesting.com
Printed in the USA
LVOW12*2236201017
553200LV00001B/5/P